"Where's you... Reese asked... where he burs... you behind the ..or and slams it in my face?"

"His job is to protect me from kidnappers, not people I choose to be with," London told him. "I still have *some* say in my life." She walked into the elegant apartment, flipping on the lights. Reese followed her in. "I made it clear that he's to perform his 'duties' tonight at a distance. Besides—" turning around, she watched him close the door "—I told him I'd be safe with you around."

Reese wasn't altogether sure about that.

He picked up a strand of her hair. The softness unsettled him. Aroused him. "And what's to keep you safe from *me?*"

She raised her eyes to his in a clear invitation. "Who says I *want* to be safe from you...?"

Dear Reader,

It's August, and our books are as hot as the weather, so if it's romantic excitement you crave, look no further. Merline Lovelace is back with the newest CODE NAME: DANGER title, *Texas Hero*. Reunion romances are always compelling, because emotions run high. Add the spice of danger and you've got the perfection of the relationship between Omega agent Jack Carstairs and heroine-in-danger Ellie Alazar.

ROMANCING THE CROWN continues with Carla Cassidy's *Secrets of a Pregnant Princess*, a marriage-of-convenience story featuring Tamiri princess Samira Kamal and her mysterious bodyguard bridegroom. Marie Ferrarella brings us another of THE BACHELORS OF BLAIR MEMORIAL in *M.D. Most Wanted*, giving the phrase "doctor-patient confidentiality" a whole new meaning. Award-winning New Zealander Frances Housden makes her second appearance in the line with *Love Under Fire*, and her fellow Kiwi Laurey Bright checks in with *Shadowing Shahna*. Finally, wrap up the month with Jenna Mills and her latest, *When Night Falls*.

Next month, return to Intimate Moments for more fabulous reading—including the newest from bestselling author Sharon Sala, *The Way to Yesterday*. Until then...enjoy!

Yours,

Leslie J. Wainger
Executive Senior Editor

Please address questions and book requests to:
Silhouette Reader Service
U.S.: 3010 Walden Ave., P.O. Box 1325, Buffalo, NY 14269
Canadian: P.O. Box 609, Fort Erie, Ont. L2A 5X3

M.D. Most Wanted
MARIE FERRARELLA

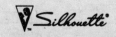

Silhouette

INTIMATE MOMENTS™

Published by Silhouette Books

America's Publisher of Contemporary Romance

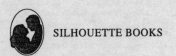

SILHOUETTE BOOKS

ISBN 0-373-27237-5

M.D. MOST WANTED

Visit Silhouette at www.eHarlequin.com

Printed in U.S.A.

Books by Marie Ferrarella in Miniseries

MARIE FERRARELLA

earned a master's degree in Shakespearean comedy, and, perhaps as a result, her writing is distinguished by humor and natural dialogue. This RITA® Award-winning author's goal is to entertain and to make people laugh and feel good. She has written over one hundred books for Silhouette, some under the name Marie Nicole. Her romances are beloved by fans worldwide and have been translated into Spanish, Italian, German, Russian, Polish, Japanese and Korean.

To
Dr. John G. Miller,
who answers all my questions,
and
is the perfect example of everything
a doctor should be

Chapter 1

There were some days that Reese Bendenetti felt as if he just hit the floor running.

This was one of those days.

He'd been up, dressed and driving before he was fully awake. Normally punctual, Reese was running behind, thanks to an asthmatic alarm clock that had chosen this morning to make a sound more like a cough than a ring when it went off. The sound had barely registered in his consciousness, and he'd fallen back to sleep only to jerk awake more than half an hour later.

When it came to getting up, Reese had been cutting time to the bone as it was, setting the clock to give him just enough leeway to shower, shave and have breakfast—provided he moved at a pace that could easily be mistaken for the fast-forward speed on a VCR.

That had been before his fateful early-morning encounter with the "little alarm clock that couldn't." Consequently, the shower had lasted all of two minutes, his hair had still been wet when he'd gotten behind the wheel of his '94 'Vette—the single indulgence he allowed himself—and his face was fated to remain untouched by a razor until he could find some time at the hospital in between rounds, emergency room patients and whatever else the gods chose to throw at him this morning.

Eating was something he couldn't think about until he came within coin-tossing distance of a vending machine at the aforementioned hospital, Blair Memorial.

Reese knew he only had himself to blame. No one had made him become a doctor, no one had told him to go into general surgery or to specialize in internal medicine. Those had been his own choices. His mother, bless her, would have been satisfied if he'd become a part-time sanitation engineer. As long as he was happy—that was her only criterion. Rachel Bendenetti never placed any demands on him, only on herself.

But healing was the only thing that did make him happy. It was in healing others that Reese felt as if he were healing himself, renewing himself. Building a better Reese Bendenetti.

He never quite understood why, he just knew that

making someone else's life a little better, a little easier, always managed to do the same for him.

That was why whenever Lukas Graywolf, a cardiac surgeon, returned to the reservation where he'd been born and raised, Reese always volunteered to go along with him and provide services to people who would otherwise not be able to afford them. The way he saw it, the rewards were priceless. It had never been about money for Reese.

He'd been enamored with medicine ever since he'd applied his first Band-Aid. Almost twenty-five years later he could still remember the circumstances. After calling him a name, Janet Cummings had turned and begun to run away, only to trip on the sidewalk. She'd scraped her knee badly and it had bled. Without hesitating, he'd run into the ground-floor apartment he and his mother were living in at the time, gotten a Band-Aid and peroxide out of the medicine cabinet—the way he'd seen his mother do—and run back outside to come to Janet's aid.

He never stopped to think that she deserved it because she'd been nasty to him, all he could think of was to stop the bleeding. Watching him, Janet had stopped crying. When he was finished, she'd shyly kissed his cheek.

Reese remembered lighting up like a Christmas tree inside. Janet had been six at the time. He'd been almost seven.

It was a feeling that he wanted to have again, and he did. Each time he worked on a patient.

Working on Tomas Morales's perforated ulcer was

a little more complex than applying peroxide and a Band-Aid to a scraped knee, but the feeling of satisfaction was still the same.

Taking off his mask, he tossed it into the hamper and sighed, bone weary. The operation had taken longer than he'd expected. As he ran a hand through his hair, holding the green cap he'd just removed in his other hand, his stomach growled. Fiercely.

"I heard that all the way over here," Alix DuCane cracked. She was standing by the sink, putting lotion on her freshly scrubbed hands. The gloves she'd just taken off chaffed her flesh. If she wasn't careful, she thought, she was going to wind up with skin like a lizard.

As if in response, his stomach growled again. One of the orderlies chuckled to himself.

Reese shrugged, tossing the paper towel he'd just used to dry his hands into the wastebasket.

"That's what happens when all you've had for breakfast is a small candy bar." It'd been stale at that, he thought. Hazards of war.

Having removed her own surgical cap, Alix shook out her short, curly blond hair as she crossed to him. "It was at least a granola bar, I hope."

Reese grinned and shook his head. "Nope. Chocolate bar. Pure sugar in a sticky wrapper. I think the candy in the vending machine down the hall is melting."

She tended to agree, having hit the machine more than once for an energy surge in the past week. Alix frowned in mock disapproval. "Shame on you, Dr.

Bendenetti. What kind of an example are you setting for your patients? You're supposed to know better.''

His shrug was careless, loose-limbed. The movement hinted that there was an ache there somewhere, waiting to emerge and make him uncomfortable. He needed a new mattress, he thought. And the time in which to purchase it.

But first things first. ''Know where I can get a reliable alarm clock?''

Alix smiled to herself. She knew of several women on staff at the hospital, including two physicians, who would have been more than happy to volunteer to wake Reese up personally, any hour of the day or night. So long as they could occupy the space beside him in the bed right before then.

There was no denying it, Alix thought, looking at her friend with an impartial eye. Reese Bendenetti was one desirable hunk, made more so by the fact that he seemed to be completely unaware of his own attributes. To her knowledge, he rarely socialized. When he did, it was to catch a beer or take a cup of coffee with a group from the hospital. Never one-on-one, except with her, and theirs was a purely platonic friendship. They had a history together, going back to medical school. He'd known her when she was still married to Jeff. Before the boating accident that had taken him away from her.

Alix knew firsthand what a solid friend Reese could be. It seemed to her that it was one of life's wastes that Reese didn't have anyone in his life who could truly appreciate the kind of man he was.

Sometimes, she mused, dedication could be too much of a good thing.

But there was still time. Reese was young. And you never knew what life had in store for you just around the next corner.

"Is that what happened this morning?" she asked as they walked out of the room connecting two of the operating rooms. He raised a brow at her question. "I happened to see you peeling into the parking lot."

Reese smiled ruefully. Driving too fast was a vice of his, and he was trying very hard to curb it.

But this morning there'd been a reason to squeeze through yellow lights that were about to turn red. He absolutely hated being late for anything, most of all his work at the hospital.

"My alarm suddenly decided to turn mute," he confessed. "I woke up fifteen minutes before I was supposed to be here."

She'd been to his apartment on several occasions and knew he lived more than fifteen minutes away from Blair Memorial.

"You can really fly when you want to, can't you?" His stomach growled again. Rotating her shoulders, Alix smiled. "Join me in the cafeteria if you feel like it. I'm having a late breakfast myself. Julie was up all night, cutting a tooth to the sound of the Irish Rovers singing 'Danny Boy.'" She'd played the CD over and over again in hopes of putting Julie to sleep. As it was she'd spent half the night pacing the floor with the eighteen-month-old. "In the meantime I'll see if I can scrounge up a rooster for you."

"You do that." But instead of following her, Reese began heading down the corridor toward the back of the hospital. "I'll see you downstairs in a few minutes," he promised. "There're some people in the E.R. waiting room I have to talk to first."

She nodded. There was protocol to follow. She knew how that was.

Her own stint on the other side of the operating arena had been a negative experience. Reese had been there with her, to hold her hand when the surgeon told her that everything humanly possible had been done, but that Jeff had still expired. Expired. As if he'd been a coupon that hadn't been redeemed in time, or a driver's license that had been allowed to lapse. Each time she'd had to face a grieving family since—which mercifully was not often—she remembered her own feelings and tempered her words accordingly. Neither she nor Reese believed in distancing themselves from their patients. That's what made them such good friends.

"I'll save a bran muffin for you," she called out to Reese.

He made a face. Bran muffins were just about the only things he didn't care for. Knowing that, Alix laughed as she disappeared.

Reese continued down the hall to the emergency waiting room area. This was the part he liked best. Coming out and giving the waiting family good news instead of iffy phrases. Tomas Morales had been to his office late last week. Choosing his words carefully, Reese had cautioned the man that playing the waiting game with his condition was not advisable. Morales hadn't wanted to go under the knife, and while Reese understood the man's fear, he also understood the consequences of waiting and had wanted to make the man painfully aware of them.

Painful being the key word here, he thought, because Morales had been in agony when he was brought into the hospital. His oldest daughter, Jennifer, and his wife had driven him to the emergency room.

This morning, as Reese had run into the hospital, he'd come through the electronic doors just in time to hear himself being paged.

And the rest, he mused, was history.

Mother and daughter stood up in unison the moment he walked into the waiting area. Mrs. Morales looked painfully drawn. There was more than a little fear in her dark eyes. Her daughter was trying to look more positive, but it was clear that both women were frightened of what he had to tell them.

Reese didn't believe in being dramatic or drawing the spotlight to himself, the way he knew some surgeons did. He put them out of their misery even before he reached them.

"He's going to be just fine, Mrs. Morales, Jennifer." He nodded at the younger woman. Jennifer quickly translated for her mother. But it wasn't necessary. The older woman understood what the look in her husband's doctor's eyes meant.

She grasped his hand between both of hers. Hers were icy cold. The woman kissed the hand that had held the scalpel that had saved her husband's life before Reese had a chance to stop her.

"*Gracias,*" Ava Morales cried, her eyes filling with tears. Then haltingly she said, "Thank you, thank you."

Embarrassed, but greatly pleased to be able to bring the two women good news, Reese gave Jennifer the layman's description of what had happened and paused after each sentence while she relayed the words to her mother. He ended by telling them that they would be able to see Mr. Morales in his room in about two hours, after he was brought up from the recovery room.

"Maybe you and your mother can go down to the cafeteria and get something to eat in the meantime," he suggested. "It's really not bad food, even for a hospital."

Jennifer nodded, her eyes shining with unspoken gratitude. Quickly she translated his words to her mother.

As he began to walk away, he heard the older woman say something to her daughter. He gathered from the intonation that it was a question.

"Please, Dr. Bendenetti, where's the chapel? My mother wants to say a prayer."

"He's out of danger," Reese assured her. Of course, there was always a small chance that things might take a turn for the worse, but the odds were negligible, and he saw no reason to put the women through that kind of added torture.

"The prayer is for you," Mrs. Morales told him halting. "For thank-you."

Surprised, he looked at her. And then he smiled. The woman understood far more than he thought.

Reese nodded his approval. "Can't ever have too many of those," he agreed. Standing beside Mrs. Morales, he pointed down the corridor. "The chapel's to the left of the front admitting desk. Just follow the arrows to the front. You can't miss it."

Thanking him again, the two women left.

And now, Reese thought as he walked out of the waiting room, it was time to tend to his own needs. His stomach was becoming almost aggressively audible. He was just grateful that it hadn't roared while he was talking to the Morales women.

He took a shortcut through the emergency area itself. As he passed the doors that faced the rear parking lot where all the ambulances pulled in, they flew open. Two paramedics he knew by sight came rushing in, pushing a gurney between them.

Instinct and conditioning had Reese taking the situation in before he was even aware that he had turned his head.

There was a woman on the gurney. The first thing he noticed was her long blond hair. It was fanned out about her like a golden blanket and gave almost a surreal quality to the turmoil surrounding her. She was young, well-dressed and conscious. And it was quite obvious that she was in a great deal of pain. There was blood everywhere.

So much for finding time for his stomach.

Reese fell into place beside the gurney. "Exam room four is free," he pointed toward it, then asked, "What happened?" of the attendant closest to him.

The name stitched across his pocket said his name was Jaime Gordon. The dark-skinned youth had had two years on the job and was born for this kind of work. He rattled off statistics like a pro, giving Reese cause, effect and vitals.

"Car versus pole. Pole won. Prettiest jag I've ever seen." There was a wistful note in his voice as he flashed a quick, wide grin. "If it'd been mine, I would have treated it like a lady. With respect and a slow, gentle hand."

It was then that the woman on the gurney looked up at him. Reese caught himself thinking that he had never seen eyes quite that shade of green, a moment before the education he'd worked so hard to attain kicked in again. He began seeing her as a physician would, not a man.

The woman was conscious and appeared to be lucid from the way she looked at him, but there was grave danger of internal bleeding. He needed to get her prepped and into X-ray as quickly as possible.

As he trotted alongside the gurney, he leaned in close to the woman so she could hear him above the noise. "Do you know where you are?"

London Merriweather's thoughts kept wanting to float away from her, to dissolve into the cottony region that hovered just a breath away, waiting to absorb her thoughts, her mind.

Ever word took effort. Every breath was excruciating. But she couldn't stop. *Don't stop. You'll die if you stop.* The words throbbed through her head.

"I know where...I'm going to be...once...Wallace...catches up to me," she answered. Her eyes almost fluttered shut then, but she pushed them opened. "Hell."

It had been a stupid, stupid thing to do. But all she'd wanted was a few minutes to herself. To be free. To be normal.

Was that so wrong?

She hadn't seen that pole. She really hadn't.

Officer, the pole just jumped up at me, honest.

Her mind was all jumbled.

It would be so easy to slip away, to release the white-knuckled grasp she had on the thin thread that tethered her to this world of lights and sounds and the smell of disinfectant.

So easy.

But she was afraid.

For the first time in her life, London Merriweather was truly afraid. Afraid if she let go, even for a second, that would be it. She'd be gone. The person she was would be no more.

She was twenty-three years old and she didn't want to lose the chance of becoming twenty-four.

And she would. If she slipped away, she would. She knew that as surely as she knew her name.

More.

Stupid, stupid thing to do. Wallace was only doing his job, guarding your body. That's what bodyguards did. They guarded bodies.

They hovered.

They ate away at your space, bit by bit until there wasn't any left.

Trying to fight her way back to the surface again, London took a breath in. The pain almost ripped her apart. She thought she cried out, but she wasn't sure.

London raised her hand and caught hold of the green-attired man beside her.

Doctor?

Orderly?

Trick-or-treater?

Her mind was winking in and out. Focusing took almost more effort than she had at her disposal.

But she did it. She opened eyes that she hadn't realized had shut again and looked at the man she was holding on to.

"I don't want...to die."

There was no panic in her voice, Reese noted. It was a bare-fact statement she'd just given him. He was amazed at her composure at a time like this.

She found more words and strung them together, then pushed them out, the effort exhausting her. She forced herself to look at the man whose hand was in hers.

"You won't let...that happen...will...you."

It wasn't a question, it was a mandate. A queen politely wording a request she knew in her heart could not be disobeyed.

Who the hell was she?

Reese had the feeling that this wasn't some empty-headed joyrider the paramedics had brought to him but a woman accustomed to being in control of any situation she found herself in.

This must be a hell of a surprise to her, then, he decided.

"No," he told her firmly. "I won't."

He noticed the skeptical look in Jaime's dark eyes, but Jaime didn't command his attention now. The young woman did.

He'd told her what she'd wanted to hear. What he'd wanted to hear, too. Because, to do was first to believe it could be done. That was his mantra, it was what he told himself whenever he was faced with something he felt he couldn't conquer.

Just before he conquered it.

The woman smiled at him then. Just before those incredible green eyes closed, she smiled at him. "Good," she whispered.

And then lost consciousness.

The next moment the rear doors burst open again. A man came running into the E.R. The unbuttoned, black raincoat he wore flapped about him like a black cape. He was at least six foot six, if not more, relatively heavyset with wide shoulders that reminded Reese of a linebacker he'd once seen on the field. The man had looked like a moving brick wall.

So did this one. And he moved amazingly fast for someone so large.

"Who's in charge here?" he demanded in the voice of a man who was accustomed to being listened to and obeyed. The next moment, not waiting for an answer, the man's eyes shifted to him. "Is it you?"

"I'm Dr. Bendenetti," Reese began.

The man was beside him in an instant. His face was pale, his eyes a little wild. Reese had no doubt that the man could probably reach into his chest and rip out his heart if he took it into his head to do so.

"This is Ambassador Mason Merriweather's daughter. I want the finest surgeons called in for her. When this is over, I want her better than new, Doctor." A good five inches taller, the man had to stoop in order to get into Reese's face. He did so as he growled, "Do I make myself clear?"

Threats had always had a negative effect on Reese. Now was no different. Disengaging his hand from the unconscious woman, his eyes never left the other man's face. They'd brought the gurney to the swinging doors of room four. He waved the team that had clustered around the rolling stretcher into the room.

When the man started to follow, Reese blocked his way, placing his hand on the bigger man's chest. There was no way he was going to allow the other man into the room.

"You'll have to wait outside while we decide what's best for her." Stepping inside, Reese turned away from the man and toward his patient.

The swinging doors closed on the man's stunned, outraged face.

Chapter 2

The next moment, the doors were pushed opened again. The bang as they hit the opposite walls resounded through the room.

"There's no way you're going to keep me out," the man informed Reese, his voice commanding even more obedience than his presence.

His hands already in surgical gloves, his attention focused on the unconscious accident victim before him, Reese's back was to the doors. He didn't even bother looking around toward the other man.

Instead, he directed his words to the dark-haired orderly on his left.

"Miguel, call security," he instructed calmly, cutting away London's suit from the site of the largest pool of blood. "Tell them to hurry."

The man stood with a foot inside the room, wavering, immobilized by indecision. A guttural sound of frustration escaped his lips. And then, struggling with his rage, his demeanor became deadly calm.

"I hope for your sake that your affairs are in order, Doctor. You lose her, you don't leave the hospital. Ever." With that, he pushed the doors apart again and stepped outside.

Rose Warren, the senior surgical nurse shivered at the quietly uttered prophesy and glanced toward Reese. "I think he means it."

"I know he does."

Reese finished cutting and examined the wound exposed beneath the blood-soaked material. There was no doubt in Reese's mind that the hulking man behind him could easily snuff out his life if he so chose, but there was no time to consider the situation. He had a patient to try to save, whether or not his own safety had just been put on the line.

He began processing the information coming at him from all sides and issuing orders in conjunction with the findings.

The man scowling just outside the swinging doors, peering through the glass and glaring at their every move, was temporarily forgotten.

The X rays confirmed what Reese already suspected. Miraculously, there were only two fractured ribs. But there was a great deal of internal bleeding going on. If the situation wasn't corrected immediately, it would turn life threatening in less time than it took to contemplate the circumstances or even to explain them to her not-so-silent guardian.

They had to hurry.

The instant the doors parted, the hulking man came to rigid attention. Surprised that they were on the move again, he fell into place beside the gurney, trotting to keep pace.

"How is she?" he demanded. "Where are you taking her?"

"There's internal bleeding," Reese told him.

He took care to keep his own reaction to the man out of his voice. Stress took many forms, and Reese figured that the man's concern might have been expressed in bullying behavior because of the nature of his work. He'd already seen the hilt of the gun the man wore beneath his overcoat and surmised that he was connected to some kind of bodyguard detail associated with the young woman. Either that or the man was her wise guy/hitman/lover.

"We have to stop it," he continued. "We're taking her to the main operating room."

As they turned a corner, Reese glanced toward the man beside the gurney. He saw deep lines of concern etched into his otherwise smooth face. His expression wasn't that of a man who was concerned about his job, but of a man who was worried about the fate of a person he cared about.

Reese wondered what the real connection between the two was and decided in the same moment that it was none of his business. All that mattered to him was doing whatever it took to save the woman's life. Anything beyond that was out of his realm.

Moving swiftly beside the gurney, Wallace Grant took London's small, limp hand into his. This was all his fault.

His fault.

Damn it, why had she driven away like that? It was almost as if she had been playing some elaborate game of chicken, daring him to catch her.

He was supposed to keep her safe, not jeopardize her life.

The ache in his chest grew. He wasn't looking forward to calling her father and reporting this latest turn of events. The man had hired him to make sure that what had happened to the Chilean ambassador's daughter didn't happen to London.

The anger was gone, temporarily leeched out, when Wallace looked up at the man he was forced to place his faith in.

"Is she going to—?"

"Pull through?" Reese supplied, guessing the end of the man's question. "I made her a promise that she would. I like keeping my promises." They'd come to another set of doors. Reese suddenly felt sorry for the man who had threatened him. For a moment the bodyguard looked like a lost hound dog. Compassion filled Reese. "You're going to have to stay outside."

Wallace didn't want to be separated. The irrational fear that she would die if she was out of his sight crowded into his fevered brain. He licked his lips as he looked past the doctor's shoulder into the pristine room that lay just beyond.

"Can't I just...?"

Reese firmly shook his head. There was no room for debate, no time for an argument. "No."

Wallace dragged his hand through slicked-down brown hair. He knew the longer he stood out here arguing, the less time the doctor had to do what needed doing. Saving the ambassador's daughter. Saving the woman he had sworn to protect with his very life.

"Okay," Wallace said breathing heavily, as if dragging his bulk around had suddenly become very difficult for him. "I'll be right out here if you need me."

"There's a waiting room," Reese said, pointing down the hall toward the cheerfully decorated area that was set aside for the families and friends of patients in surgery.

"Right out here," Wallace repeated, stationing himself in the corridor against the opposite wall. From his position he would be able to look directly into the operating room.

Reese shrugged. "Suit yourself."

Maybe the man *was* a relative, Reese thought. Or connected to the woman on some level that went far deeper than first noted. Or maybe the man was one of those people who took their jobs to heart. If so, Reese couldn't fault him. He fell into the same category himself.

The next moment Reese entered the operating room, and all extraneous thoughts about missed breakfasts, silent alarm clocks and strange personal connections were left out in the corridor.

Along with the man with the solemn face and worried eyes.

Three hours later it was over.

The freshly made openings had all been sutured closed, the bleeding had been stopped, the ribs had been taped. She wasn't, as her bodyguard had demanded, better than new, but she would be well.

The woman's vital signs had never faltered once. They'd remained strong throughout the lengthy procedure, as if her will to live was not to be snuffed out by whatever curve life and the road had thrown at her.

He wished all his patients were that resilient.

Weary, hungry, relieved, Reese stripped off his surgical mask and cap for the second time that day. Now that this newest crisis was over, he became aware again of the deep pinched feeling in his gut. It felt as if his stomach was stuck to his spine. He still hadn't had a chance to take in anything more substantial than a stale candy bar.

This time, he promised himself, he didn't care if the paramedics brought in Santa Claus and his eight tiny reindeer laid out on nine stretchers, he was determined to go get something to eat before he literally passed out from hunger.

At this point freshness would no longer play a part

in his selection. He didn't care what he ultimately got to eat. His only criterion was that it remain relatively inert long enough for him to consume it.

Even the bran muffin was beginning to sound pretty tempting.

But first, he knew, he had to go out and face the sentry out in the hall. The man who had remained steadfast throughout the entire procedure, standing there like an ancient gargoyle statue, guarding the door and watching the surgeon's every move. Reese hadn't had to look up to know that the deep-set brown eyes were taking in everything that was being done in the small, brightly lit operating room.

"How—" The single word leaped out at him as soon as Reese pushed open the door.

"She's fine," Reese said quickly, cutting the man off. He didn't want to stand around for any more threats or whatever it was that the man had in mind now that the operation was over. "Like I said, she had some internal bleeding, but we found all the openings and sutured them. She had a couple of fractured ribs as well—"

Wallace stopped him right there. "Fractured?" he demanded. "You didn't mention them before."

Reese chose to ignore the accusatory note in the other man's voice. Instead, he cut him some slack. It was pretty clear that they were both a little over-wrought, he thought.

"It could have been a great deal worse. The paramedic who brought her in said her car was totaled."

Reese saw guilt wash over the wide face. Had that somehow been his fault? he wondered.

"Yeah, it was." And then, just as suddenly, the guilt left his eyes. His expression turned stony. "How soon can she be moved?"

"Why don't we wait and see how she does first?" Reese calmly suggested. The next twenty-four hours would decide that. "In the meantime, maybe you should go to admitting and give them any information you can about her. Administration has forms to keep your mind busy for a while."

"I don't need to have my mind kept busy," the man snapped.

"But I do." With that, Reese turned on his heel and began to walk away.

"Hey, Doc."

For a moment, Reese debated just continuing to walk away. There was no sense in encouraging any further confrontation. But if there was going to be another scene, he might as well get it over with now.

Suppressing a sigh, Reese half turned and looked at the larger man. "Yes?"

There was what passed as a half smile on the man's face. He suddenly didn't look the least bit threatening, but more like an overgrown puppy whose limbs were too big for his body.

"Thanks."

Surprised, it took Reese half a beat to recover. He nodded. "It's what I do."

Mercifully, Reese's stomach had the good grace to

wait until he was well down the hall before it let out
with a fearsome rumbling.

Each eyelid felt as if it was weighed down with its
own full-size anvil.

Either that, or someone had applied glue to her
lashes.

Maybe they should apply the same compound to
the rest of her, London thought giddily, because she
felt as if she had shattered into a million pieces.

A million broken, hurting pieces.

Breathing was almost as much of a challenge as
trying to pry her eyes open. It certainly hurt a great
deal more.

And right now there was a herd of drunken African
elephants playing tag and bumping into one another
in her head.

London heard a deep, wrenching moan echoing all
around her, engulfing her. It sounded vaguely familiar.

It took her a beat to realize that the noise had come
from her.

The pain was making her groan. And why did it
feel as if there was a steel cage wrapped around her
upper torso?

London opened her eyes or thought she did. The
only thing that seemed to be filtering through was
white. Lots of white.

Heaven? It didn't feel hot, so it couldn't be hell.

No, it felt cool, very cool.

Was she dead?

Where was the light everyone had always talked about? The light that was supposed to lead her to a better place. Or was that just a lie, a myth like unconditional parental love?

She thought she heard a male voice.

St. Peter?

Lucifer?

Batman?

Her mind jumped around from topic to topic like a frog attempting to reach safe ground using lily pads that kept sinking beneath his weight.

The male voice spoke again. This time she heard real words. A question. "How are you feeling?"

Was he talking to her?

With one last massive effort, London concentrated on pushing her lids open. This time she succeeded and saw—a man.

Not Batman, Superman, she amended. No cape, no blue tights that showed off rows of muscles, but definitely Superman. Right down to the chiseled chin and blue-black hair falling into brilliant blue eyes.

She swallowed. Her throat felt like rawhide. He'd asked her something. What? London searched the vacant caverns that comprised her mind and finally found the words, then laced them together.

Feelings, he'd asked something about feelings. No, wait, he'd asked her how was she feeling, yes, that was it.

It was a damn stupid question. How did she look? If she looked half as bad as she felt, Superman had his answer without her saying a word.

"How are you feeling?" Reese repeated for the third time.

He bent over close to her so she could hear him. He had been in twice before, only to find her still sleeping. This time, as he'd checked her chart, he saw her eyes flutter slightly. She was trying to come to.

London took a breath before answering. It felt like someone had shot an arrow into her ribs. "Like…I've been…run over…by…a…truck."

Was that breathy, scratchy voice coming out of her? It didn't sound like her, London thought. She tried to read Superman's face and see his reaction to the pitiful noise. Was he recoiling in horror?

No, his eyes were kind. They were smiling.

She liked that. Smiling eyes.

"Not quite a truck," Reese told her. "They tell me a pole did this."

The single word brought with it a scene from somewhere within her brain. She and her parents, sitting at a long, white table, watching blond girls in native costumes with wide skirts, black corsets, red boots and wreaths of flowers in their hair, dancing.

Poland, her parents and she had been in Poland.

Poland, the last place her mother had been before she couldn't be anyplace at all.

"Pole?" she echoed. She didn't remember hitting a Polish national.

Reese saw the confusion in her face and wondered if she was suffering a bout of amnesia. Her airbag had failed to deploy and she'd hit her head against the steering wheel. Amnesia wasn't unheard of.

"The one you tried to transplant by running into,"
he told her gently, taking her pulse. The rhythm was
strong. She had a good constitution. Lucky for her.
"The paramedic almost wept over your Jaguar."

The words were filtering into her brain without en-
countering matching images. Her jaguar. A pet cat?
No, car, her car. The man was talking about her car.

Oh God, now she remembered. It all came rushing
back at her as fast as she had raced her car to get
away from Wallace.

She'd lost control and totaled her beautiful car.

London groaned, the loss hitting her between the
eyes—the only spot on her body that didn't hurt.

She raised her eyes to look at him as he released
her wrist. "Is it totaled?"

"Like an accordion."

The paramedic, Jaime, was still shaking his head
and talking about the colossal waste of metal to anyone within earshot. He drove a small, secondhand foreign car whose odometer had gone full circle twice,
and he looked upon the other vehicle as if it was a
gift bestowed by the gods. He periodically drooled
over Reese's Corvette.

Reese studied London's pale complexion for a moment. There was a bandage on her forehead where
flesh had met wheel, but apart from that, she was a
gorgeous woman, possibly the most perfect specimen
he had ever seen. She could have been forever disfig-
ured. Why had she risked losing all that in the blink
of an eye?

"What were you trying to prove?"

"Nothing," she answered quietly. She would have turned her head away if the effort hadn't hurt so much. So she just looked at him steadily, meeting his probing gaze. "Just looking for space."

He laughed shortly under his breath. The woman had intelligent eyes, and she certainly didn't look stupid, but then, looks could be deceiving.

"You very nearly got it. Six feet by six by six," Reese told her, pausing to write a notation in her chart. "A final space in the family plot."

Beside her mother, she couldn't help thinking. Maybe it would be peaceful there and she could finally find out who she was.

A flicker of rebellion rose from some faraway quarter that hadn't been banged around relentlessly, and London looked at her intrusive surgeon with as much defiance as she could muster.

"A lecture? Save your...breath, doctor...I've heard...it all. "

She'd certainly heard more than her share. From her father, from Wallace, although she preferred the latter because at least Wallace was her friend. Her father, well, she didn't really know what Ambassador Mason Merriweather was or how he figured into her life, other than to impose restrictions on her for as long as she could remember. Even Wallace and the other two bodyguards, Kelly and Andrews were part of her life because of him.

"Not a lecture, a fact," Reese told her mildly. He slipped her chart back into its slot at the foot of her bed.

She was tired, very tired and there was this wide, soft, inviting region just waiting for her to slip into it. Its pull was becoming irresistible, but London struggled to ask one more question.

"Did you do it?"

The question caught him off guard. Reese looked at her. She appeared to be drifting off again. In another moment she'd be asleep, and the keeper at the gate would have to continue to wait before he would have the opportunity to talk with her.

"Do what?" Reese asked.

Every word was a struggle. Her mind was shutting down again. "Save…my…life."

What he had done was utilize his training, his education and his instincts, not to mention the up-to-date technology that a hospital like Blair Memorial had to offer. There was no doubt in his mind that twenty years ago she would already have been dead. But even now, with all this at his disposal, there remained at bottom the x-factor. That tiny bit of will that somehow triumphs over death.

He allowed himself a small smile, though he doubted she could even detect it. "You saved your own life. I just put the pieces together."

"Modest." The single word came out on a labored breath. "Unusual…for…a…man."

He began to say something in rebuttal, but it seemed that at least for now, his side wasn't to be heard. His patient had fallen asleep again.

Just as well, Reese thought, standing at the foot of the bed and regarding her for one long moment. He didn't feel like getting embroiled in a debate right now.

Not even if the opposing team looked like an angel. An angel, he mused, slipping out of the room, who had gotten banged up falling to Earth.

Very quietly he closed the door behind him.

Chapter 3

The moment Reese stepped out of the ICU, he found himself accosted by the big man who had stood vigil in the hallway all this time. He'd been told that Wallace Grant had been hovering around the nurses' station ever since London had been brought out of recovery. To his credit, he had tried not to get in anyone's way.

The question in the man's eyes telegraphed itself instantly to Reese.

"She's asleep," Reese told him.

Wallace frowned as he sighed, frustration getting the better of him. He'd already put in a call to London's father. The ambassador was scheduled for a meeting with a highly placed official in the Spanish government, but he'd canceled it and was catching the first flight from Madrid to LAX that his secretary could book for him. Wallace wanted to have some good news to give the man who signed his paychecks when he arrived.

Laying a large paw on Reese's shoulder to hold him in place, Wallace blocked his exit.

"Is that normal?" he wanted to know. "I mean, shouldn't she be waking up around now?"

Reese knew for a fact that the man had been looking in on London for his allotted five minutes every hour on the hour. The day nurse had told him so. But it was obvious that each time he did, he'd found the young woman unconscious.

"She did," Reese told him. Surprise and relief washed over the other man's face, followed by a look of suspicion. Wallace was a man who took nothing at face value. "For about five minutes," Reese elaborated. "She's going to be in and out like that for most of the day and part of tomorrow." Very deliberately he removed Reese's hand from his shoulder. "Maybe you should go home."

Wallace looked at him sharply. "And maybe you should do your job and I'll do mine." Wallace didn't appreciate being told what to do by a man who knew nothing about the situation they were in. "Her father pays me to be her bodyguard. I can't exactly accomplish that from my apartment."

Reese didn't care for the man's tone or his attitude. "Seems to me you didn't 'exactly' accomplish it earlier, either, and you were a lot closer then."

To his surprise he saw the anger on the other man's face give way to a flush of embarrassment. His remark had been uncalled for. Reese chastised himself; he was civilized now, at least moderately so, and was supposed to know better.

He chalked it up to his being tired. It wasn't an excuse, but it was a reason.

"Sorry," Reese said. "I didn't mean that the way it sounded." He wasn't up on his celebrities, but it seemed to him that someone so young wouldn't normally need to have her own bodyguard. Her name didn't ring a bell for him, but that, too, was nothing new. For the most part, except for his small circle of friends or his mother, he tended to live and breathe his vocation. "Why does she need a bodyguard?"

The wide shoulders beneath the rumpled brown jacket straightened just a fraction. That was all there was room for. The man had the straightest posture he'd ever seen outside of a military parade, Reese thought. He'd had Grant pegged as a former military man.

"You can ask her father that when he gets here," Wallace told him, his tone formal. "It's not my place to tell you."

Guarded secrets. Definitely a former military man, Reese decided. He shrugged. Whether she had a bodyguard or not didn't really matter to him, as long as the man stayed out of the way.

"Just an idle question. Don't have time for many of those," Reese confessed, more to himself than to the man in front of him. Before he left, he stopped at the nurses' station and looked at the middle-aged woman sitting behind the bank of monitors, each of which represented a patient on the floor. "Page me if the patient in room seven wakes up." He leaned in closer to her and lowered his voice. "And don't forget to tell our semifriendly green giant here, too."

Slanting a glance at the man who had resumed his vigil in the hallway, the strawberry blonde raised a silent brow in Reese's direction.

He grinned. "Call it a mercy summoning," he told her just before he left.

Reese was in the doctor's lounge, stretched out in a chair before a television set showing a program that had been popular in the late eighties. He must have seen that particular episode five times, even though he'd rarely watched the show when it was originally on. *Murphy's Law.*

He wasn't really watching now, either. The program was just so much white noise in the background, as were the voices of the two other doctors in the room who were caught up on opposite sides of a political argument that held no interest for Reese.

For his part, Reese was contemplating the benefits of catching a quick catnap, when his pager went off.

Checking it, he recognized the number. He was being summoned to the ICU. He wondered if the nurse was just responding to his instructions, or if London had taken a turn for the worse.

"No rest for the wicked," he murmured under his breath. Rising, he absently nodded at the two physicians, who abruptly terminated their heated discussion as they turned toward him in unison.

"Hey, Reese, you up for a party tonight?" Chick Montgomery, an anesthesiologist who knew his craft far better than he knew his politics in Reese's opinion, asked him enthusiastically. "Joe Albright's application to New York Hospital finally came through, and he's throwing a big bash at his beach house tonight to celebrate."

His hand already on the door, Reese shook his head. He didn't feel like being lost in a crowd tonight. He had some serious sleeping to catch up on. "I'm not planning to be upright at all tonight."

The other doctor, an up-and-coming pediatrician, leered comically. "Got a hot date? Bring her along, the more the merrier is Joe's motto, remember?"

Reese didn't even feel remotely tempted. "No hot date," he told them. "I'm booking passage for one to dreamland tonight. Maybe I'll actually manage to start catching up on all the sleep I lost while I was in med school," he cracked.

That was the one thing he missed most of all in this career he'd chosen for himself. Sleep. When he was a kid, weekends were always his favorite days. He'd sleep in until ten or eleven, choosing sleep over watching early Saturday-morning cartoon programs the way all his friends did. Sleep had been far more alluring.

It still was.

Trouble was, he didn't get nearly enough anymore. He couldn't remember the last time he'd gotten a full night's sleep. If anything, life after medical school had gotten even more hectic for him. There was always some emergency to keep him at the hospital or to drag him out of bed early.

You asked for it, he thought, walking down the first-floor corridor toward the front of the building.

The ICU was located just beyond the gift shop. As he passed through the electronic doors that isolated the intensive care unit from the rest of the hospital, Reese absently noted that the hulking guardian wasn't hovering around in the vicinity.

He wondered if the man had finally decided to take a break and go home for a few hours. Diligence could only be stretched so far.

"Jolly green giant on a break?" he asked Mona, the strawberry blonde who'd paged him.

The woman shook her head and pointed toward room seven.

Apparently, Reese thought, diligence could always be stretched just a wee bit further. The man he'd just asked about was now hovering over London Merriweather's bed. To his surprise the booming voice the bodyguard had earlier used on him had been replaced by a voice that was soft and pleading.

A gentle giant, Reese mused. Who would have thought it?

"Promise me you won't do that again, London," he was saying. "I'm only here to look out for you. I'm the good guy."

London only sighed in response, but to Reese it sounded like a repentant sigh. But then, maybe he was reading things into it. He didn't really know the woman. She might just be placating the big guy.

Sensing his presence, Wallace glanced toward the door. The look he gave Reese clearly labeled him as the intruder, rather than the other way around.

Since only five minutes at an ICU patient's bedside was allowed, Wallace had taken to peering periodically into London's room when the nurse's back was turned. Each time he did, he saw that London was still sleeping. His agitation grew with each unfruitful visitation. As did his concern.

So when he'd looked in this time and found that her eyes were open, his heart had leaped up like a newly released dove at a wedding celebration. He'd lost no time in coming in and peppering the young woman for whose safety he was responsible with questions and admonishments.

"You gave me some scare," he'd freely confessed, saying to her what he would never have admitted to another man. "When I saw your car hit that pole, I thought my heart stopped." A small smile had curved his lips. "I found out I still remembered how to pray."

She'd looked at him ruefully then and he could see that she was sorry. When she had that look on her face, he couldn't bring himself to be angry with her, even though they both knew that she'd pulled a stupid stunt by taking off at top speed like that, trying to lose him. London was alive, and that was the bottom line. That was all that counted. The rest could be worked out somehow. He'd make sure of it.

Wallace had said his piece and didn't want London to be upset, with him or with herself so he'd smiled shyly at her and added, "Bet the Big Man Upstairs was surprised to hear from me after all this time." He'd placed his hand over hers, dwarfing it. Letting her know that he would always be there for her. That there was nothing to be afraid of. "But you're going to be okay. The doc who operated on you told me so."

She'd nodded, as if she knew she was going to be all right. Because Wallace had told her so. "Sorry. I just wanted to get away."

And he'd looked at her, his dark eyes pleading once more. The next time could prove fatal. "Not from me, London. Not ever from me. I'm not just your body-guard, I'm your friend. I'm the guy who's supposed to keep you safe, remember?"

She'd bitten her lip and nodded. He'd almost gotten her to promise never to take off like that again when the doctor had walked in on them.

Self-conscious about his lapse in protocol, Wallace quickly lifted his hand from London's.

"She woke up," the bodyguard told him. There was a touch of defensiveness in his voice, and the soft tone Reese had heard just a moment earlier was completely gone, vanishing as if it had never existed.

Reese nodded as he approached the bed. "So I see."

His eyes shifted to the woman in the bed. He looked at her with a discerning eye. London still looked very pale, but there was a brightness in her eyes that had been absent earlier. She was definitely coming around, he thought.

"Let me check your vital signs." Reese's tone was light, conversational as he took the stethoscope from around his neck and placed the ends in his ears.

"Vital signs all present and accounted for, Doctor," London cracked. She would have saluted him, but her arms still felt as if they each weighed more than a ton.

"You don't mind if I check for myself." He picked up her wrist and placed his fingers on her pulse. Mentally he began counting off the seconds and beats.

"Feel free." She watched him for a moment. He looked so cool, so calm. Was that just a facade? What did it take to light a fire under him? "Did you know that in some cultures, if you save a person's life, that life belongs to you?"

His eyes met hers briefly. "Makes a casual birthday present seem a little ordinary and rather insignificant, doesn't it?"

Taking a pressure cuff that was attached to the wall, Reese wrapped it around her arm, then increased the pressure until the cuff was tight along her arm. This was something the nurses did periodically, but he liked checking for himself. Nothing like hands-on experience whenever possible.

He kept his eye on the readings as the air was slowly let out. Her blood pressure was excellent. And she was no longer speaking in fragments, which meant that she wasn't having trouble taking in deep breaths. She had amazing recuperative powers.

Satisfied, he removed the cuff, then made a notation in her chart. He was aware that the giant standing on the other side of her bed was watching his every move. "How do you feel?"

She almost felt worse than when she'd first come in on the gurney. But then, she reminded herself, she'd probably been in shock.

"Like Humpty-Dumpty."

He laughed under his breath. "Well, lucky for you we're staffed with something other than all the king's horses and all the king's men." He smiled at her. "So we were able to put Humpty-Dumpty together again." Reese replaced the cuff in its holder on the wall. "Your vital signs are all strong. You keep this up and you can move into the suite that Grant, here—" he nodded at the giant "—insisted on reserving for you."

He was referring to one of the rooms located in what the hospital staff referred to as the tower. Large, sunny rooms that could have easily been mistaken for hotel suites, made to accommodate VIPs who came to the hospital with their own entourages. CEOs, movies stars and, on occasion, politicians made use of the suites whenever circumstances forced them to stay at the hospital.

At present only one of the four rooms was in use. While checking London in, Wallace had insisted on reserving the largest suite for her once she was well enough to leave the ICU. The tab had begun the moment he'd made the request formally.

London tried to raise herself up on her elbows and discovered that it was yet another stupid move. Pain shot all through her, going off through the top of her head. She winced and immediately chastised herself. She didn't like displaying her vulnerability.

Reese was at her side, adjusting the IV drip that was attached to her left hand. "You feel pain, you can twist this and it'll increase the medication dosage."

She frowned. "I don't do drugs."

"You do for the moment," Reese informed her mildly, stepping back.

London sighed. All she'd wanted was a little control of her life, and now look—she was tethered to a bed, watching some clear substance drip into her body and listening to an Ivy League doctor tell her what to do.

She looked at him. "I don't want a special room. I want to go home."

"Then you shouldn't have tried to break the sound barrier using a Jaguar," Reese informed her mildly, ignoring the glare that was coming from the woman's bodyguard. He replaced her chart, then sank his hands deep into the pockets of his lab coat as he regarded his newest patient. He offered her what he deemed was his encouraging smile. "We'll try not to keep you too long."

She sighed. It was already too long. She knew it was her own fault, but that didn't change the fact that she didn't want to be here. That being in a hospital made her uneasy, restless. She wanted to get up out of bed, walk out the door and just keep walking until she hit the parking lot.

But being tethered to an IV and feeling as if she

had the strength of an anesthetized squirrel wasn't conducive to her going anywhere. At least, not for the moment.

She tried to shut out the sadness that threatened to blanket her.

"I called your father." Wallace had been wrestling with the way to tell her since he'd put through the call to the embassy.

They both knew he had to, but he also knew how much she didn't want him to make the call.

London sighed again, more loudly this time. Great. This was just what she needed on top of everything else. To experience her father's disapproval coming down from on high. They hardly had any contact at all, except when her father felt the need to express his disappointment about something she'd done or failed to do.

In the past year she had turned her hand—and successfully at that—to fund-raising for charities. There hadn't been a single word of commendation from her father even though the last affair had raised so much money that it had made all the papers.

She looked at Wallace. She had thought she could trust him. In the past eighteen months, while he'd been heading the security detail for her father that she thought intruded into the life she was still trying to put together, they had become friends.

Obviously, salaries transcended friendships.

"Why?" she asked sharply. "There's no point in worrying him."

Wallace didn't care for the fact that the doctor was

privy to this exchange, but he had no say in the matter. Reaching for the newspaper section that was folded and stuffed into his overcoat pocket, he tossed it onto her bed.

"He'd be plenty worried if I hadn't. This was on the bottom of page one in the *L.A. Times*. I figure a story just like it is bound to turn up in the papers or on the news in Madrid." The small brown eyes bored into her. "You know how much your father likes to watch the news."

Almost against her will she looked at the paper. Ambassador's Daughter Nearly Killed In Car Accident.

London frowned. Stupid, stupid. She shouldn't have given in to impulse. But she'd been so tired of having her every move shadowed, of feeling isolated but not alone.

"Yes, I know." Well, there was no undoing what she'd done. She was going to have to pay the piper or face the music or something equally trite. London pressed her lips together. Her eyes shifted toward Reese. "Wallace, I'd like to talk to the doctor alone."

Wallace opened his mouth in protest. The doctor should be the one to leave, not him. But there was clearly nothing he could do. Reluctantly he inclined his head. "I'll be right outside."

Because none of this was his fault, London mustered a smile, resigning herself to the inevitable. And, she supposed, in light of everything, there was a certain comfort in knowing Wallace was around. "Yes, I know."

"Right outside," he repeated, this time for Reese's benefit just before he left the room.

For a moment there was no sound except the gentle noises made by the machines that surrounded the upper portion of her bed, monitoring her progress, assuring the medical staff that all was going as it should.

Reese had places to be, patients to see. He didn't have time to dance attendance on a headstrong young woman who hadn't learned how to curb her desire for speed. "You wanted to say something to me?"

"Yes." She'd never been very good at being humble. Maybe because it made her feel as if she were exposing herself, leaving herself vulnerable.

Finally she said, "Thanks."

She made it sound as if it pained her to utter that, Reese thought. "Like I said earlier, it's my job. And if you really want to thank me, get better." Finished, he began to walk out.

"I don't like hospitals."

The statement came out of nowhere. Stopping just short of the door, Reese turned around to look at her.

For some reason she suddenly looked smaller, almost lost in the bed. He remained where he was. "Not many people are crazy about them," he acknowledged. "But they serve their purpose."

She knew that. Knew that she'd probably be dead if Wallace hadn't summoned the paramedics to get her here in time. But that still didn't change the feelings that were clawing inside of her.

"My mother died in a hospital," she told him quietly.

Reese took a few steps toward her bed. "I'm sorry to hear that."

She barely heard him. Only the sympathy in his voice. She didn't know doctors could be sympathetic. She thought they were supposed to be removed from things like death. "In Brussels. It was a car accident. She wasn't even thirty."

Each halting word brought the incident closer to her. Standing alone on a hospital floor with a large, black-and-white checkerboard pattern, feeling abandoned. Feeling alone. Watching a tall man in a white lab coat talking to her father. Watching her father's proud, rigid shoulders sag. Wanting to reach out to him in her anguish, but being restrained by the woman who had been placed in charge of her.

Something started to make a little sense. "Is that why you—"

She wasn't going to come up with any analogies. She had no death wish. She had a life wish. She wanted to find one. A life she could be content with, if not happy. "No, I was just trying to get away."

He glanced toward the closed door. "From the jolly green giant?"

Wallace was harmless, even though he was an expert marksman and had been the head of security for Donovan Industries before being wooed away by her father when her old bodyguard had retired.

She shook her head and instantly regretted it. "From being London Merriweather, Ambassador Mason Merriweather's wild daughter." That was how her father thought of her, she knew. And how the headlines had once viewed her.

She didn't seem so wild right now, Reese thought. She looked almost frail and vulnerable, although he had a feeling she wouldn't appreciate that observation. "Simpler ways of doing that."

The streak of rebellion that had become her constant companion since the day she lost her mother raised its head at his words. "Such as?"

Seemed obvious to him. "Such as you could do away with the wild part."

Everyone seemed to have an opinion on how she was to live her life. "Will this lecture be itemized on the hospital bill, or does it fall under miscellaneous?"

He had better things to do than spar verbally with a spoiled brat who happened to be very, very lucky as well as extremely gorgeous.

"It falls under common sense." Reese turned and once again began to walk away. "You might think about getting some."

"I don't like people who insult me," she called after him.

He stopped by the door. "And I don't like people who are careless with their lives. Especially when they have everything to live for."

Where did he get off, saying things like that to her? He knew nothing about the pain in her life. Nothing about the emptiness. "How would you know that?"

Reese didn't know why he was bothering. Except that she was his patient and she was in pain. Pain that went deeper than the lacerations and bruising she had sustained in the crash.

"Because most people have everything to live for, Ms. Merriweather. The alternative is rather bleak and, to my knowledge, completely nonreversible."

With that he left the room.

Chapter 4

He'd almost lost her.

For a long moment, his soul troubled, he stared at the mural that dominated one wall of the small studio apartment where he lived. The mural was comprised of all manner of photographs in all sizes, both black-and-white and color. There were newspaper clippings, as well, though those were few.

His eyes lovingly caressed the face he saw before him. The photographs were all of the same woman.

London Merriweather.

London, the daughter of the ambassador to Spain. The daughter of the former ambassador to England. It was there that she was born twenty-three years ago.

Returning to the task that he had begun, he shook his head in mute sympathy as he cut out the latest clipping from the *Times*. It was a relatively small article describing the accident that had almost taken her out of his world. He had larger articles, and better pictures, but he kept everything, every scrap, every word, every photo. They were all precious.

Because they were all of her.

What kind of father names his daughter after a place he's living in? he wondered not for the first time. After something that was associated with his line of work? Where was the love there?

It was simple. There wasn't any.

Her father couldn't love her the way he could. The way he did.

No one could.

He tossed aside the newspaper, smoothing out the clipping he'd just liberated from the rest of the page.

Very carefully he taped the clipping with its accompanying photograph in one of the last free spaces on the wall.

The mural was getting larger. It was taking over the entire wall.

Just like his feelings for London were taking over everything in his life. His feelings were evident in every breath he took, every thought he had. They all revolved around London, around his possessing her.

Loving her.

She was going to be his.

Some way, somehow, she was going to be his. He knew it, sensed it, felt it in his very bones.

He just had to be patient, that was all. Once she realized, once she saw how much he loved her, how he could make her happy, she would be his. And everything would be all right again.

He sat down in his easy chair and felt her image looking at him from all angles, all sides. He returned her smile, content.

Waiting.

The feeling of oppression hit Reese the moment he stepped off the elevator onto the top floor of the hospital tower.

He was already annoyed. He didn't get that way often, but having his professional authority circumvented was one of the few things that was guaranteed to set him off. His orders had been countermanded by the hospital chief administrator, Seymour Jenkins, because Mason Merriweather had come in and demanded that his daughter be taken out of the ICU and placed in the tower suite that the head of London's bodyguard detail had already reserved for her.

Granted, the woman was getting better and he was about to order the transfer of rooms himself, but he didn't appreciate being second-guessed, or more to the point, ignored, because a VIP was on the scene making demands.

Seymour Jenkins didn't ordinarily interfere in any of his doctors' cases, which was what made this such a complete surprise.

He'd looked infinitely uncomfortable when Reese had burst into his office after having gone to the ICU and found London's bed vacant.

"I would have understood if you'd needed the

bed,'' he'd told Jenkins. ''But it was empty. Why the hell did you move my patient without first checking with me?''

A dab of perspiration had formed on Seymour's upper lip. He'd run his hand nervously through the thin strands of his remaining hair. ''The ambassador got on the phone himself—''

Reese watched the man's Adam's apple travel up and down his throat like a loose Wiffle ball.

''And what? He threatened to huff and puff and blow the hospital down if you didn't instantly obey him and put her in the tower suite?''

Jenkins rose from his desk and crossed to Reese in an effort to placate him. He was more than a foot shorter than the surgeon. ''Please, be reasonable. Look at it from my point of view. Ambassador Merriweather is an influential man, he has connections, and we're a nonprofit organization—''

Why did things always have to come down to a matter of money rather than ethics and care?

Thinking better of approaching him, Jenkins decided to keep a desk between them. ''I've never seen you like this,'' the man protested nervously.

Even though not completely seasoned, Reese Bendenetti was still one of the finest surgeons on the staff at Blair Memorial, which was saying a great deal. The ninety-year-old hospital, which had recently undergone a name change from Harris Memorial because of the generous endowment from the late Constance Blair, prided itself on getting the best of the very best. The last thing Jenkins wanted to do, for the sake of the hospital's reputation as well as for practical reasons, was to alienate the young physician. But neither did he want to throw a wrench into possible future contributions from the ambassador and any of his influential friends.

"There's a reason for that. I've never been completely ignored before." Reese leaned over the desk, bringing his face closer to the other man's. "She's my patient, Jenkins."

The man drew himself up, finding a backbone at last, albeit a small one.

"Yes, and this is my hospital—and yours," he pointed out. "Ambassador Merriweather is a former captain of industry." Merriweather's company had made its mark on the stock market before he had resigned from the board to take on the responsibility of a prestigious foreign embassy. "He hobnobs with kings and presidents, not to mention some of the richest people in the world. We can't have him unhappy with us," Jenkins insisted. "Besides, we're not endangering his daughter with the transfer." He'd made a point of checking the Merriweather woman's record—after the fact. "You noted yourself in her chart that her progress is amazing. And we sent up monitors with her, just in case."

Which in itself had probably required a great deal of juggling, Reese surmised. He had said nothing in response to the information meant to placate him. Instead he'd turned on his heel and walked out, heading straight to the tower elevators and straight to London's floor.

Where the wall of noise hit him.

The area appeared to be in the middle of being cordoned off. Men in gray and black suits were everywhere. Reese looked sharply at the nurse who was sitting in the nurses' station.

"What the hell is going on?"

The older woman turned her head and covered her mouth so that only Reese could hear. "Ambassador Merriweather's landed, and from the looks of it, he's brought half his staff with him."

He could see that. That still didn't answer the question. "Why?"

The woman shrugged her wide shoulders. This was causing havoc on her usually smooth-running floor. "Something about keeping his daughter safe."

Reese felt his anger heighten. Maybe he was overreacting. His quick temper went back to the days when he was growing up and was regarded as someone from the wrong side of the tracks, someone whose opinion—because his mother's bank account was represented by a jar she kept in a box beneath her bed—didn't count. But if his patient's life was in jeopardy from something other than the injuries she'd sustained the other day, someone should have taken the time to inform him.

"What room did you put her in?"

The nurse didn't even have to look. "Room one." She pointed down the hall toward where the activity grew more pronounced. "The largest of the suites."

He was vaguely familiar with it. He remembered

thinking that the room was somewhat larger than the first apartment he'd lived in.

Reese nodded his head and made his way down the corridor.

Besides being on the cutting edge of medicine, Blair Memorial prided itself on being uplifting and cheerful in its choice of decor. The tower rooms were designed to go several steps beyond that. Here patient care was conducted in suites that looked as if they were part of an upscale hotel rather than a hospital.

Reese supposed there was no harm in pandering to patients who could afford to waste their money this way, as long as playing along didn't get in the way of more important matters, such as the health of the patient.

As he approached suite one, a tall, unsmiling man stepped forward, his hand automatically reaching out to stop Reese from gaining entry to the room he was guarding.

"I'd put that hand down if I were you," Reese told him evenly. He'd had just about enough of this cloak-and-dagger VIP nonsense.

Wallace turned from the man he was instructing to see what was going on. Recognizing Reese, he crossed the room to him. "He's okay," he told the bodyguard who was part of his detail. "He's the main doc." His brown eyes shifted to Reese. "This is Kelly. He's on midnight to eight," he stated matter-of-factly.

"Well I'm on round-the-clock when it comes to my patients," Reese replied. He looked at Kelly coolly, waiting. The latter dropped his hand and stepped out of the way.

But as Reese started for the unblocked door, Wallace shook his head and moved to stop him.

"I wouldn't go in there just yet if I were you," he advised.

Was someone in there, brightening up her room, giving her a pedicure? He was in no mood to be dealing with the very rich and their self-indulgence.

"And why not?"

Wallace glanced toward the door, lowering his voice. "The ambassador's in there. He's talking to London, and I think they'd rather keep it private."

Wallace was willing to place bets that London did. If he knew her father, the man was probably giving her a dressing-down for being so reckless. For his part, Wallace would have liked to be there to shield her, but it wasn't his place and he knew it. Still, he couldn't help but feel sorry for her.

It was going to take more than a private chat between the ambassador and his daughter to keep Reese out. He figured he'd wasted enough time as it was.

"I'll keep that in mind," Reese said to the other man as he walked by London's primary bodyguard and into the room.

Mason Merriweather narrowed his piercing blue eyes. He wasn't happy about this. Not happy at all.

He had no idea what to do with her.

Damn it all, being a father shouldn't be this difficult, especially at his age.

He could negotiate contracts and peace treaties that were advantageous to people on both sides of the table, get along in several languages with a host of people and was known for his ability to arrange compromises and defuse the hottest of situations, be they global or, as they were once upon a time, corporate.

But when it came to his own daughter, he hadn't a clue how to behave, what to do, what to say.

It was his considered opinion that he and London had never gone beyond being two strangers whose photographs just happened to turn up in the same family album.

Perhaps part of the problem was that she behaved and looked so much like her late mother. It was like receiving a fresh wound every time he laid eyes on her. Because London made him think of Anne, and Anne wasn't here anymore.

She hadn't been for a very long time.

And now this, a car accident that brought all the old memories back to haunt him. Because Anne had died behind the wheel, taking a turn on a winding road that hadn't allowed her to see the truck coming from the opposite direction—the truck that had snuffed out her vibrant young life and taken the light out of his own.

Anne had never gotten the hang of driving on what she termed the wrong side of the road. And it was he who had paid the price for that.

But now it was London, not Anne, who was the problem. Just when he thought she was finally settling down. After all, she'd acquiesced to his wishes re-

garding the bodyguard detail. He'd thought—
hoped—that this was a sign that she was finally coming around, finally learning not to make waves in his
life.

He should have known better.

The initial words between them when he'd walked
into the room had been awkward. They always were.
She looked a great deal more frail than he'd thought
she would. The IV bottle beside her bed, feeding into
her hand had thrown him.

Anne had looked that way. Except her eyes had
been closed. And she was gone.

But London wasn't. Thank God.

"How are you feeling?" he managed to ask in a
tone he might have used to an underling or even a
complete stranger.

"Achy."

London waited to see a sign of some kind of emotion from the man she felt kept himself so tightly
under wraps he could have easily passed for an an-
droid...or a mummy.

The ambassador had just endured the long plane
ride from Madrid to John Wayne Airport with the
specter of his daughter's imminent death sitting beside him. Seeing her alive had been a relief, but it
was instantly replaced by a feeling of helpless anger.

Throwing decorum to the winds, thinking that he
could just as easily have been attending London's funeral right now as standing by her bedside, he demanded hotly, "What the hell were you thinking?"

She wanted comfort, she wanted to hear him say

that he was glad she was alive. Not recriminations. But then, after all this time, she should have known better. He hadn't been there when her mother, her whole world, had been taken from her. He hadn't held her, comforted her, cried with her. And she'd been a child then. She was a woman now. Why did she expect him to do things differently?

Her eyes narrowed just the way his did. "I was thinking that I wanted to get away from the bodyguard. That just for once I wanted to be me, driving alone without leading a wagon train through the streets. Is that so much to ask?"

His anger rose at the accusation. He knew she thought it was all his fault. As if he had been the one to kidnap the other ambassador's daughter. Didn't she realize that he was doing this just to keep her safe? That she meant everything to him?

"We've been through this, London," he said sternly. "These men are here for your own protection."

She touched the bandage on her forehead and thought of the one taped to her ribs. She raised her eyes to challenge her father. "Didn't do a very good job, did they?"

It took everything Mason had to keep his temper. He wasn't going to shout at her. He didn't believe in shouting. Shouting was for lowlifes, and he had always striven to raise himself above his own roots.

Spreading his thumb and index finger he smoothed down his pencil-thin mustache. It was still dark, even though his hair had turned silver gray years ago. He liked to joke that he owed the change in color to London. Right now he figured it wasn't that far from the truth.

"They would have, if you didn't travel around thinking you were the reincarnation of James Dean, bent on tearing around the countryside."

"I wasn't tearing, I was driving," she snapped.

It was hard to defend a point when she knew she was wrong and would have admitted it freely if only he cared about her.

Why couldn't her father have just come up and hugged her? Told her that he'd been worried sick about her when he'd gotten the news? Instead he was carrying on nobly, descending on her with his entourage.

Damn it, just once couldn't he be her father instead of the ambassador?

Mason sighed. This was getting them nowhere. Nobody could ever tell her what to do, and she'd only gotten worse with age. "Look, I don't want to argue about this. I've decided to have you transferred to another hospital—"

Just like that. Without asking, without consulting. He was treating her like a child. Just the way he'd sent her away to boarding school right after her mother's accident. Instead of trying to make things better, he'd only made them worse. Made her feel more isolated, more alone.

And more brokenhearted.

Well, she wasn't eight years old anymore. He

couldn't do with her as he willed just because it was more convenient for him.

"No."

He looked at her sharply. Why couldn't she just accept things for once instead of fighting him at every turn? "London—"

But she didn't let him get started again. "You've already had me transferred to another room. I'm not playing musical hospitals. The care is good—my doctor is the best, they tell me. I'm staying here."

His voice rose almost against his will. "For once in your life, London, stop fighting me just for the sake of fighting."

Reese picked that moment to walk in.

London's eyes darted toward him, and he saw the momentary flicker of distress there. Maybe he was crazy, but it felt as if she was asking him to come to her aid. He couldn't help wondering if she even knew that plea was in her eyes.

Or maybe it was all in his mind.

"You're upsetting my patient, sir," Reese said, crossing to the bed. "If you can't refrain from doing that, I'm going to have to ask you to leave."

Mason drew himself up to his full height and squared his shoulders. He was somewhat heavier than the man who was challenging him and only half a head shorter. "Do you know who you're talking to, young man?"

Reese never missed a beat as he applied the blood pressure cuff to London's arm. "Yes, someone who's upsetting my patient, and I can't have that."

Mason wasn't accustomed to being addressed this way. He'd been an ambassador for more than thirty years and was always treated with the utmost respect. He'd become used to being listened to and obeyed—except by London.

"I am her father."

"Yes," Reese said mildly, noting the reading he was getting. "I know. That might be a contributing factor to your daughter's reaction, but I don't have time to explore that right now." He replaced the cuff back in its position. "Mr. Merriweather—"

"Ambassador Merriweather," Mason corrected him tersely.

He was never one for titles, but he obliged. "Yes, well, Ambassador, your daughter's not supposed to be agitated this way. It'll impede the progress she's making." He looked at the older man pointedly. "So I suggest that if you have anything else to tell her that will upset her—you keep it to yourself for the time being."

Color crept up the man's aristocratic cheekbones. "I don't appreciate being spoken to in this fashion."

Taking London's hand, Reese placed his fingers over her pulse and mentally counted out the numbers. Her heartrate was higher than it had been. Undoubtedly because of her father's presence.

"No, I don't suppose you do, sir, and I don't particularly enjoy speaking this way myself, but my patient comes first, above and beyond family ties, charitable contributions or political standings." He released London's hand, still looking at the ambassador. "Am I making myself clear?"

He succeeded in unsettling the ambassador. It took the older man a moment to get his bearings. When he did, he slanted a look toward London, then one in Reese's direction.

"I would like to speak to you alone, Doctor—" Mason paused to read Reese's name tag, then raised his eyes to the younger man's face "—Bendenetti."

Reese inclined his head and allowed himself to be led to a corner of the suite. This had better be good, he thought.

"If I find that your care of my daughter is lacking in any manner, *any* manner, you'll have me to answer to, personally, and I guarantee it will not be a pleasant experience."

Reese had no doubt about that at all. But he didn't like being threatened by the ambassador any more than he had liked it when the bodyguard had done it. "I'll have myself to answer to first, Ambassador. My patients receive my full attention and the best care I can offer them, regardless of their standing in the community or," he added pointedly, "any threat that might be issued."

Reese didn't add that in his short career he had already been threatened graphically with vivisection by the brother of one of his patients. It had been in Los Angeles, and the man had been the head of a local gang in the area. He had gone into great detail about what would happen to the surgeon in charge of his sister should she die on the operating table.

Reese deliberately went and opened the door. He held it, looking expectantly at Mason. "Now if you'll excuse me, I have to examine my patient."

Curbing his anger but admiring the spirit that had caused the younger man to stand up to him, Mason inclined his head then looked toward his daughter. "We're not finished yet," he told her, raising his voice. "I'll see you later."

With that he walked out.

London watched the door close. She couldn't remember anyone ever putting her father in his place. "I guess that makes twice you've rescued me. Keep this up and you won't be able to get rid of me."

If she meant that as a threat, even in jest, it didn't have the desired effect, because he could think of things that were a great deal worse than having a beautiful woman in his life, even one who was emotionally wounded, as this one apparently was.

"Do you know that you're the first man who's ever put my father in his place?"

Reese picked up her chart again and read the various notations by the day nurses.

"Wasn't trying to do that, I was only trying to get him out of my face—" Reese looked up from the chart and at her "—and yours for the time being."

"I appreciate that." She smiled at him, and much to his surprise, he realized that his own pulse had stepped up just a tad.

Chapter 5

"You're not getting enough sleep."

Reese smiled at the woman sitting opposite him in the tiny breakfast nook of the house he'd bought for her. He supposed, no matter how old he got, his mother would always fuss over him.

It didn't bother him. In a way he had to admit that there was comfort in knowing that some things remained the same, year in, year out. This was a far cry from the way he'd felt in his teens, when everything his mother said was guaranteed to irritate him, even though he knew he was being unreasonable.

But in the past ten years or so, he and his mother had settled into a pattern mimicking the one that had been in place when he was a boy. The only difference now was that they were individuals rather than a set—

independent yet forever bound by mutual affection and caring. He wouldn't have it any other way.

Reese finished off the piece of French toast he was nibbling. Taking breakfast together once a week was a tradition his mother had begun years ago, when both their schedules were hectic beyond belief. He still liked keeping it up.

"Mom, that's the kind of thing I'm supposed to say to people."

Just barely into her fifth decade, Rachel Bendenetti was still an attractive woman by anyone's standards. Her dark hair had a few streaks of gray, but her skin was still smooth and her eyes were as lively as ever. She was a woman who enjoyed life no matter what curves it threw at her.

She turned those lively eyes on her only son now as she slipped another piece of French toast onto his plate.

"Ever hear the one that goes Physician, Heal Thyself? They're not hinting that he should perform surgery on himself, Reese. Just see to his own needs." Her eyes narrowed as she refreshed his empty cup with aromatic coffee, then tended to her own. "Just the way you should."

He took his coffee black, his optimism light. He laughed before taking a sip. "And put you out of business?"

Rachel became serious. She knew he didn't take advice, but she was bound to try. He was working long hours at the hospital and keeping up with his own private practice. That amounted to burning the candle at both ends. Granted, she'd done it herself for far less pay, but that was her and this was Reese. The difference to her was enormous.

"There's no reason for you to work yourself into a frazzle, Reese. You're not the only surgeon around."

He drained his cup and placed it back on the table. "Yes." Rising, Reese pretended not to notice that there was a new piece of French toast on his dish. He was stuffed as it was. Outside of these once-a-week get-togethers, breakfast was a haphazard affair that was comprised of anything coming out of his refrigerator, taken cold. "But I am one of the best."

"*The* best," she corrected firmly and with a great deal of motherly pride, "but that's not going to do anyone any good if you're dead."

Coming around the table, Reese bent over and kissed her cheek. "That's what I love about you, Mom, your flair for drama."

She wasn't sure if he was referring to what she'd just said or to her concern for him, but she honed in on the latter. "No, I'm just looking out for my only son." She pushed aside her own half-empty cup. There was time enough for coffee later, before she went to the shelter. "Take some time off, go on vacation." As long as she was shooting for the moon, she might as well go all the way. "Meet a girl. Make me a grandmother."

So that was where this was headed. Amused, Reese shook his head. "You're too young."

Rachel rose to her feet. "True," she allowed, her eyes sparkling. "But you're not."

He'd never taken a real vacation, nothing beyond a couple of days off here and there. The week he'd been off when he'd had that miserable strain of flu didn't count. Vacations held no allure for him. He liked his work. But to placate his mother he said, "I'll think about taking some time off after I discharge London Merriweather."

About to pick up her plate and take it to the sink, Rachel paused, thinking.

"Where have I heard that name before?" And then, before he could tell her, she suddenly looked at Reese sharply as it came back to her. "The newspaper. I just read about an accident—" Her eyes widened considerably. "You don't mean that the ambassador's daughter is—"

Not his mother, too, he thought, nodding in response. "My patient. They brought her in on my shift."

Without saying another word, Rachel hurried into the next room, which was officially the small, formal dining room. It was also where she kept all the previous days' newspapers until they were picked up for recycling once a week.

Reese heard her searching through the pile. Triumphant, she returned a minute later, a four-day-old A section of the *L.A. Times* in her hand.

"*This* ambassador's daughter?" Rachel pointed to the article at the bottom of the first page.

"That ambassador's daughter," he acknowledged.

Taking the paper from her, Reese glanced at the article. It was the morning edition, and it carried an old photograph of London. She'd worn her hair differently then, he noted, and the photo was grainy. But even the newsprint couldn't detract from the sparkle that seemed to be in her eyes. It was there even when she was angry, the way she'd been when her father had descended on her.

Funny how some things just stuck with you, he thought, handing the paper back to his mother.

Rachel folded it and left the section on the table. "And she's your patient."

A deaf man would have picked up on the wonder in his mother's voice. What was it about these people that caused others to be in awe of them?

"We just established that, Mom." He raised a brow. "Or should I take you in for short-term memory-loss testing?"

With an exasperated squeal, Rachel swatted at him, then looked thoughtfully down at the photograph. "Very pretty girl." She glanced up at Reese. "Article doesn't say anything about a fiancé."

He knew that look. It meant his mother was delving further. It also meant he should get going.

"Far as I know there isn't one. At least, none that I've seen or heard her mention." Because he knew he probably wasn't going to get a chance to stop for lunch, he picked up his glass of orange juice and finished it off. Putting the glass down again, he gave his mother a warning look. "Drop it, Mom."

She couldn't have looked more innocent if she'd

been created five minutes ago. "Drop what, dear, the paper?"

The paper was already on the table. And her meaning was out in the air. "The thought."

Her eyes widened further, though it was hard to keep her lips from curving and giving her completely away. "What thought?"

He tapped her forehead with his fingertip. "The one I can see forming in your mind." They'd always been close, he and his mother, and he almost always knew what she was thinking. And right now she was being a very typical mother. "She's my patient."

Rachel grinned. It was an expression that succeeded in transforming her into someone who looked as if she was far too young to have a son as old as Reese. "Exactly."

He took out his car keys. "And there's such a thing as ethics—"

But Rachel was way ahead of him on that score. "She won't always be your patient. That's the beauty of your being a surgeon. You operate, you check, you release." Rachel dusted off her hands. "And then she's not your patient anymore." She looked back at the thumbnail-size photograph again and smiled. "Really lovely girl. Needs a strong hand, though, according to what I read in the article. Just a little too headstrong." Rachel looked up at her son. "Is that true?"

He thought of London's standoff with her father and the way she tried to maintain her own space within the fishbowl existence that she'd had. You could call that headstrong, he thought. Or you could call it determined to be her own person. Either way, he had no desire to get into that kind of a discussion with his mother right now. Given an inch, he knew she'd be trying to invite the woman over for dinner.

"Don't believe everything you read," was all he said. He began to head for the door. "Gotta go, Mom. Thanks for breakfast."

Placing his dish beside hers on the counter, Rachel turned and accompanied him to the front door. "Maybe what she needs is a good home-cooked meal."

Reese nearly laughed. He'd seen it coming a mile away, he thought. "Maybe."

His mother looked at him brightly. "I cook. At home," she added.

Crossing through the small living room, Reese opened the door. "Hence a home-cooked meal, yes, I know." He made an elaborate show of looking at his watch. "Gotta go, really. It's getting late."

It was not even 7:00 a.m., but she knew he had rounds to make before he went to his office and he was nothing if not conscientious.

Still, she didn't want to give up on this totally. She had a feeling about it. Or maybe she just wanted to have a feeling. "I don't need much notice," she persisted.

"Yes, I know. Ready for anything, that's you."

Opening the door, Reese stopped, realizing that must have sounded flippant. He knew how much this woman had given up so that he could pursue his own dreams. His mother could have remarried, could have been assured of security years before he'd grown up and been able to give it to her. Joe Abernathy had asked her to marry him twelve years ago. Reese knew that she'd loved the man. But Joe had not wanted to be saddled with a child and had wanted her to send him off to a good military school. He could have afforded the best.

She hadn't even taken any time to think it over. She'd refused, and she and Joe had eventually come to a parting of the ways. She'd continued to hold down two jobs so that he would never lack for anything, not even her. Looking back, he didn't think she'd slept much in ten years. His mother was his first experience with a superwoman.

Impulsively, even though he wasn't given to being demonstrative, Reese hugged her to him.

"Thanks, Mom."

Surprised, delighted, it took Rachel a second to collect herself and return the embrace. She felt tears betraying her as they sprang to her eyes. She loved him dearly and, more than anything in the world, she wanted him to be happy.

"Don't be such a stranger," she said as her son released her. "I make other things than breakfast, you know."

Shaking his head, Reese laughed as he walked away. "Yes, I know."

Rachel Bendenetti stood watching her son as he got into his car and drove away. Mentally she crossed her fingers and offered up a few prayers to any saint in the immediate vicinity who had the time to work a miracle or two. She wasn't partial to a particular saint; she appealed to them all. The only thing that interested her at the moment was the end result.

"He's a good boy," she said out loud, although she knew there was no need. There were tallies of these things somewhere. Every good deed was noted and remembered. She figured that her son had a huge volume with his name on it. "It's time he had something more than his medical books to curl up with. See to it," she instructed as she walked back into the house.

She had every hope that she wasn't going to be ignored. After all, it wasn't as if she was always asking for things.

It seemed to Reese that each time he walked into her room, London Merriweather looked a little better, a little more attractive.

The spark in her eyes was the first thing to return, then the color in her cheeks.

Four days into her stay, she'd done something with her hair. At first he'd thought that maybe her father had sent in a hairdresser for her. Under the circumstances, it wouldn't have surprised him. But Betty at the nurses' station on this floor had said that one of the nurses had helped London into the shower and to blow-dry her hair.

The end result was that when he walked in this morning, it took him a moment to remember just what he was supposed to be doing here. He blamed it on his mother, on some kind of posthypnotic suggestion she had probably planted in his brain.

But he still had trouble drawing his eyes away...still had to remind himself that London was his patient and that was all.

London was sitting up in bed, reading, looking like a vision.

She had on an ivory peignoir with lace trim around a scooped-out neckline that flatteringly emphasized her breasts. Her shoulder-length golden-blond hair formed a cloud around her and seemed to sparkle in the morning sunlight that came in through the windows.

The moment he walked in, she raised her head. The preoccupied look on her face faded, to be replaced with a warm, inviting smile.

She closed her book and let it fall on her lap. "Enter, Daniel."

He remember that he was supposed to be able to walk and crossed to her bed. He looked at the title of the book. The words were in red letters, but didn't register. "Daniel?"

Amusement entered her eyes as she slowly nodded her head. The woman knew exactly the kind of power she had and how to wield it, he thought.

"The man who bearded the lion in his den and lived to tell about it."

He forced himself to mentally take a few giant steps back—and to remember that she was his patient and only that. He picked up her chart, though he didn't open it. "You consider yourself a lion?"

London laughed. Tigress, maybe. But not a lion. "Not me, my father." She studied him for a moment. Definitely good lines. She wondered if he was the least bit impressed with her. Or was he one of those equality advocates who was put off by wealthy, powerful people? She didn't blame him. She felt a little that way herself, even though she'd grown up with them all around her. "He respects you, you know."

Reese remembered the way her father had glared at him, and the warning he'd issued. He figured that London was fabricating things. "How can you tell?"

She indicated the bed and the room. "Because I'm still here."

He took no credit for that. Because he found himself in danger of staring into her liquid green eyes and getting lost there, he looked down at her chart and flipped it open to the last page.

Reese allowed himself a mild smile. "I thought that had more to do with your refusal to leave."

"The ambassador doesn't listen to me and no one tells him what to do unless he is inclined to do it, anyway." She debated keeping the next thing to herself, and then decided to tell him to see his reaction. You could tell a lot of things about a person by his reaction to having his privacy invaded. "He's had you checked out, you know."

Reese didn't care for that, but there was nothing he could do about it. He made an entry in her chart. "I never doubted it."

Because she was curious herself, she'd made Wallace give her that report. The bodyguard hadn't seemed comfortable about releasing the information to her, but she'd overruled him. Wallace was a pussycat. "You graduated at the top of your class."

Reese spared a single glance in her direction. "It was a dirty job, but someone had to do it." With that he placed her chart back in its slot at the foot of her bed. Suite or no suite, some things remained the same.

London cocked her head, looking more closely at the man who she'd dreamed about last night. A very hot, erotic dream that had made her look at him more closely now. It seemed that her subconscious was way ahead of the game. And right on target.

She also noted something else. "You look tired."

The comment surprised him and then he laughed quietly. "My mother said the same thing this morning."

It was still early, that meant he'd had to have come from there. "You live with your mother?" He didn't seem the type.

Was she trying to pigeonhole him, he wondered. "No. Stopped by for breakfast."

"A good son," she approved mockingly, then her tone faded as a question entered her mind, ushered in by a wave of sadness and longing. "What's it like?"

He wasn't following her. Looking at her, he saw that the flippant expression was gone. He couldn't quite fathom the one he saw. "What's what like?"

She supposed he'd probably think she was a loon, but he'd brought it up in the first place. "Having breakfast with your mother?"

Reese remembered she'd said that her mother had

died in a hospital. "A lot like this—toast mixed with interrogation. Except that we had French toast."

"Your favorite?"

There was a small shrug. "She likes to make it, I like to eat it."

Noncommittal, she thought. Like most of the people who drifted through her life. She made sure of that. With people who were noncommittal, there was never the danger of wanting to commit to them. You knew where you were at all times. There was no fear of being abandoned, of being left behind. That you would part was a given to begin with.

London laughed, but he could hear a sad echo within the sound.

He came closer to her. "How old were you when your mother died?"

She raised her eyes to his, surprised at the personal question. He didn't strike her as the type to ask. Part of her was happy he did. "Eight."

Reese nodded, taking the information in. He could visualize her, the girl she'd been. Something tugged on his heart. "Rough. I was ten when my father left."

"Left?" She hadn't thought of him having anything but a perfect background, a perfect family. A mother who made breakfast for her busy, successful son and a father who liked to brag about him to his friends, whose chest puffed up at the mention of his son's name. To find out otherwise was surprising.

He'd divorced himself a long time ago from any pain associated with the incident. Even when his father had been there, he hadn't really *felt* like a father.

Just a man who lived with them. Who lost himself in a bottle whenever the whim hit.

"Just like that," he told her. "One morning he decided he didn't want to be a family man anymore. Didn't want the responsibility of taking care of a wife and son, not that he really did much of that, anyway," he said more to himself than to her.

His words replayed themselves in his head, surprising him. He generally didn't talk about personal matters, not to the small circle of people he considered his friends, and certainly not to strangers. Maybe it had been the look in London's eyes that had prompted him to share this darker side of his life. She looked as if she needed comforting, even though her mother's death had happened so far back in her past.

London curbed the impulse to place her hand over his. "I'm sorry."

He shrugged. "Nothing to be sorry about. I think in the long run we got along better without him, although my mother had to take on two jobs to make ends meet."

Earning his own way had made him strong. She should have realized that. It had done the same for her father. Except it had worn away any kindness he might have possessed.

"We never had that problem," she told him honestly. "Ours was bigger."

The bewildered expression on his face urged her to explain.

"Your father's leaving brought you and your mother closer together. My mother's 'leaving,'" she said, using a euphemism, "drove my father and me farther apart. He sent me off to boarding school right after the funeral."

Just the way Joe had wanted to do with him, Reese thought. The empathy was immediate, but because it made him feel slightly uncomfortable, he said, "He was probably doing what he thought was best."

"Yes, for him." There was a trace of resentment in her eyes when she looked up at him. "You see, even then I looked like my mother."

"She must have been a beautiful woman." The words came out before he could stop them.

London looked at him in surprise and then smiled. "Why, Doctor, is that a compliment?"

Her smile was seductive, there was no other word for it. Any more than there was a way to immunize himself against its effects.

Still Reese tried to make his voice sound cool, distant. "I don't give compliments as a rule. I make observations."

She laughed lightly. She'd embarrassed him; she could see that. "What a lovely observation, then." Making up her mind, she scooted to the edge of the bed, then dangled her legs over the side. She winced a little as she did so.

No pain, no gain.

Reese was at her side immediately, taking her hand. "What are you trying to do?"

She wiggled down a little more, trying to get her feet to touch the floor. Getting out of bed now was a far cry from the bouncing exit she was accustomed to.

"I'm supposed to get out of bed and walk a little before breakfast." She looked at him deliberately. "Doctor's orders."

Yes, he knew. They were standard orders. He hesitated a moment. "You could wait until after breakfast."

But London was already wrapping her fingers around his hand tightly as she continued to slowly draw herself out of bed. Her legs felt incredibly wobbly. Just as wobbly as they had the night before when she had attempted a constitutional with the night nurse.

But the sooner she was moving, she thought, the sooner she would return to her life. It was important to her to take back control—what control she'd had—of her life.

She almost fell as she tried to steady herself.

He caught her, wrapping his arms around her just as she was about to sink to the floor.

London looked up at him. "Why wait?"

He felt his heart throbbing in its newfound position: his throat. Maybe this wasn't such a good idea. But then, if he backed away, she would ask why. And see the reason no matter what excuse he tendered.

This morning there was no surgery to claim his attention—barring anything that might be going on in the emergency room. And he had never been a coward. "Once around the corridor?"

She brightened. "That's my goal."

"Admirable." He took her hand and slowly led her out the door.

He caught the reflection of her smile in the windowpane as they passed and felt as if he'd been pierced by an arrow.

Reese shut away the thought, refusing to explore it. He was going to have to make certain that he gave his mother a different topic to occupy her mind the next time he stopped over for breakfast.

Chapter 6

With no undue conceit Reese prided himself on being reasonably intelligent. Added to that he was a physician, a surgeon. He figured that meant he was capable of recognizing electricity when he came up against it. Whether it turned up at the end of a live wire or in the unexpected contact between two people, he knew electricity when he felt it.

He felt it now.

As London took another faltering step forward, she suddenly dipped beside him. He'd only had a light hold of her hand. Instantly his arm went around her waist, drawing her to him and steadying her before she had a chance to sink down completely.

It was the second time in as many minutes that their bodies had touched.

The current that traveled along his at the sudden

contact was enough to light up one hotel in Las Vegas for an entire month. Possibly longer.

This jolt was stronger than the one before.

Startled, wondering if he was hallucinating, Reese looked at London in surprise as he gently raised her up. The look in her eyes told him he wasn't the only one who had found himself standing in the middle of an open field during an electrical storm with a lightning rod in his hand. She was as surprised, as affected, as he was.

Careful, Bendenetti, you don't want to do anything dumb, he warned himself sternly. Allowing whatever the hell it was that was now racing through his veins to take even infinitesimal control of him would be dumber than dumb. It would also be asking for trouble with a capital *TR.*

Reese took a better hold of London's hand, offering her steadfast support as she struggled to stand up. Maybe his mother was right at that, he thought. Maybe he really needed to get out once in a while. He knew biology, knew that man did not live on work alone.

The problem was he had no time for anything else. Not if he was going to continue to build up an excellent reputation. It was Reese's avowed goal to become one of the top surgeons in the state, not because of any egotism or need for adulation on his part, but because he'd always believed that if you undertook something, you should do it to the very best of your ability.

And along with an excellent reputation came the monetary compensation that would enable him to pay his mother back a small portion of what she'd sacrificed for him over the years. He knew no matter what he did, he could never fully repay her, but at least he could make a dent in his debt.

Damn, London thought, but she hated feeling as if a strong wind could whisk her away with no trouble at all, and silently cursed her own weakness. It had been four days since the accident—wasn't she supposed to be on her way to recovery by now?

And what was this other thing that was going on? This tension, this static charge dancing between them? What was that all about?

Taking a step, her fingers tightened around the doctor's, as if she could somehow channel his strength into her legs. He had very strong hands, she thought, yet they weren't large.

Gentle hands. Like the hands of a lover.

London bit her lower lip, exasperated, refocusing. "How long before I stop doing sudden imitations of a rag doll?"

She sounded annoyed with her progress. He had a feeling she had no patience with weakness, her own especially. London's impatience didn't come as a surprise to him. Given her nature, he'd expected it.

They took another step together toward the door.

"Seems to me that you're doing very well now. Better than expected."

She allowed herself to slant a glance in his direction before looking back at the floor and her feet. "In general…or better than expected of a pampered ambassador's daughter?''

There was a defensive edge to her question that surprised him. It made him wonder about the kind of life she'd led until now. He forced himself to concentrate on her steps and not on any extraneous thoughts he was having, or the fact that her nearness was affecting him in ways that had no place here.

"In general," he replied, keeping his voice mild. "Maybe I'm wrong, but I get the distinct impression that the pampering you're being subjected to is being done against your will."

He was rewarded with a smile that flashed at him like diamonds. It lit up her eyes and made her even more beautiful.

"Handsome, skillful *and* astute," she noted approvingly. "Why hasn't some woman snapped you up, Reese?"

He'd forgotten she had access to the information her father had an investigator gather about him. That gave her an advantage he didn't care for. All he knew about London was what was in her chart. He wasn't obsessively private, but he didn't particularly care to have his life an open book, either.

"Maybe we'd get along better if you called me Dr. Bendenetti," Reese suggested pointedly.

Well, that put her in her place, London thought. "Ah, barriers, I can relate to that. All right, *Dr.* Bendenetti," she said. "Why haven't you become some lucky lady's trophy?"

They were almost at the door leading to the corridor. "Too busy."

Though it irked her, she paused for a moment to gather her strength. "Too busy to enjoy yourself, or too busy to be tied down?"

His eyes met hers. She was sharp. And into nuances. "Both. And you'd do better to concentrate on your situation, not mine."

His hand against the door, Reese pushed it open. He found himself looking up at the bodyguard who was standing directly in front of the doorway.

"I'll take over from here, Doc." The big man's tone was friendly enough, but there was no room for argument. The bodyguard wasn't making a suggestion, he was stating a fact.

Not that Reese had any intention of opposing him. He had other patients to see, and besides, he had a feeling that it was safer all around if he just surrendered London into the man's waiting arms.

But if the two men were in agreement, London was not. She made no effort to take the arm he offered, but kept hers firmly through Reese's.

"That's all right, Wallace. *Dr.* Bendenetti wants to make sure I'm not doing anything that might impede my progress." She smiled as she added, "But you can watch if it'll make you feel better about doing your job." She turned her face toward Reese. "Ready, *Dr.* Bendenetti?"

Reese noted that she deliberately emphasized his name and title every time she said it.

The right thing to do, he knew, was to hand her

off to the hulking bodyguard. Reese had no idea why he acquiesced to her wishes.

Maybe it was because deep down they were his wishes, too. Which made even a stronger argument for his not spending any more time than he had to with this headstrong woman.

But, he reasoned, there was absolutely no opportunity for anything remotely improper to occur. They were under the hawklike gaze of the bodyguard, who gave no indication of turning his attention to anything else, and there was a smattering of hospital personnel milling around. He was safe.

From her and himself.

So Reese inclined his head and gave in. "All right, just once up and down the hall," he agreed.

It was London's natural tendency to balk at restrictions, and she particularly disliked being treated like an invalid. "Oh, but I can do more."

He had no doubt that she could. Much more. Some of it even involved walking. But he didn't think he could afford to allow her to spread her wings beside him. Not while she was his patient. The lady was far too tempting. Reese had always had a very healthy sense of self-preservation. Doctors who became involved with their patients never went far, and deservedly so. He didn't intend to have his name mentioned among the number.

"No point in tiring you out." His tone put an end to the debate. "Ready?"

She nodded, her face turning toward the corridor. Determined. She let him win this round. "Ready."

They took baby steps that he could see irritated her even though she was the one who set the pace.

Her frown deepened with each step she took until he finally asked, ''What's the matter?''

She huffed impatiently. ''I'm used to sprinting, not crawling.''

At least, mercifully, she didn't have to drag around her IV bottle with her anymore, London thought. But she'd expected, once that was a thing of the past, to be making greater strides. Instead she wasn't striding at all.

Reese was accustomed to exercising patience. She obviously was not, he thought. ''You have to crawl before you sprint. And when you get discouraged, just think they could be saying words over you right now, sinking your casket into the ground.''

Her eyes on the ground, monitoring her own small steps, London shook her head.

''Not me.'' She gritted her teeth together. Her ribs ached with every step she took, every movement she made. Wasn't that supposed to be a thing of the past by now?

Reese looked at her. ''You're never going to die?''

''No.'' It was getting harder now. She didn't risk looking at him, only the floor. ''Never going to be buried,'' she clarified. ''When I go, I want to be cremated. Have my ashes scattered to the wind from the highest point in the country.'' She allowed herself an enigmatic smile. ''That way I can live forever.''

''Interesting thought.'' He watched her put her feet down. She was slow, but she wasn't walking on glass.

Which meant that either she was getting better at tolerating pain or the pain was receding. "Which country?"

"What?" Glancing at him, she'd thrown herself off and had to stop for a second. "Sorry," she muttered.

He waved a hand at her apology. She expected perfection from herself, he thought. He expected to find perfection in books, not in life. At least, not in his life.

"From what I've gathered, you've traveled all around the world. I was just wondering which country you'd picked to scatter your ashes in."

London didn't even have to pause to think. There was no hesitation.

"This one." She saw him glance at her, mild surprise on his face. "The other places are all right to visit, but this is home." It always had been, in her mind. She was just an American girl, happiest when she was here. "My mother's buried here. In San Clemente," she added, then flushed. "Guess this a rather a morbid topic to be discussing in a hospital."

He made no comment. The hospital was like life. All about living. And dying.

She was breathing harder and they had yet to reach the end of the corridor. "Want to stop?" he suggested, concerned.

"No." She turned her face toward him proudly before resuming the snail's pace toward the end of the corridor. "I'm a very stubborn woman."

He stuck his tongue in his cheek. "Really? I hadn't noticed."

Wise guy, she thought. Exhausted, she looked to see how much farther she had to go. Too far.

"Another thing you might not have noticed, they've stretched out the hallway since yesterday."

He nodded, playing along. "It's what happens when they steam clean the rugs. The carpet doesn't keep its shape." He looked at her, sympathy getting the best of him. Pushing herself was only good for so long, then it became damaging. "We can stop. I can get a wheelchair for you." There was one down at the end of the hall. He indicated it.

"No." She squared her shoulders, though the movement cost her, telegraphing sharp pain through parts of her body. "You can use the wheelchair if you like. I did this yesterday, I'm doing it today. I'm not about to slide backward."

He couldn't help but admire her.

It gave him something else to think about rather than the electricity that insisted on humming between them like a haunting refrain.

"Made it," she sighed as they reached the end of the corridor.

"Now we go back," he told her, his voice deliberately light.

She responded with something under her breath he didn't quite catch. He thought it better that way.

In the interest of getting through this, Reese kept her arm tucked through his, his hand wrapped around her fingers and his pace achingly slow. Eventually they made it back to Wallace, who had been intently watching their every step, like a chaperon out of an eighteenth-century novella.

"She looks tired." The comment was made to Reese. Wallace's tone was accusatory.

She'd never liked being fussed over. Now more than ever she felt as if it cut into her space.

"There's a reason for that." London sighed and looked longingly toward the bed that was all the way over against the opposite wall in her suite. "I think I've had enough for now." She didn't want Reese to think of her as a weakling. "Maybe I'll do more later."

"No maybe about it," Reese informed London, escorting her back into the room. He could almost feel Wallace's displeasure as the latter fidgeted a step behind them, then halted at the doorway, sensing that he wasn't needed or wanted. "The more you walk, the faster you can get out of here."

She smiled, her relief growing with each step she took toward her bed. She spared a glance toward the doctor. "Anxious to get rid of me?"

The tension shimmering between them didn't abate. "You said you hated hospitals," he reminded her.

A few more steps. Just a few more steps, she cheered herself on. She could do this—even though the idea of turning to the doctor and asking him to carry her the rest of the way was not without appeal. With her luck he'd probably tell Wallace to take over for him. "You pay attention."

He saw her smile blooming and tried not to dwell

on it. "It's my job. I believe in the whole picture, not just a section."

Almost there.

Her knees were beginning to feel as if they wanted to buckle again. She willed them not to. "So, I'm more to you than just taped-up ribs and a bruised liver?"

Reese realized that he didn't want her to be, but she was a damn sight more than that. And he had a feeling that she knew it.

"Yes," he answered simply. "If you treat the whole person, the whole person gets well faster." He swept away the cover and gently lowered her onto the bed. She released an unguarded sigh as she made contact with the mattress. Without thinking, he removed her slippers and raised her legs onto the bed, then covered her.

The look of gratitude she gave him went straight to his gut. He chastised himself for his reaction. It changed nothing.

She'd never known that a bed could feel so wonderful. For a moment, London just allowed herself to enjoy the sensation. Then she looked toward Reese. "Admirable philosophy, *Dr.* Bendenetti."

He wondered if she was going to continue to emphasize his title, or if she would tire of the game. In either case he had to get going. Reese crossed to the doorway. "I'll see you later."

London sighed, a touch of restlessness already setting in. "I'm not going anywhere."

But apparently he was.

The moment Reese stepped out of the suite, Wallace took him by the arm, stopping him. Now what? "Something you want, Grant?"

"Not me, the ambassador," the bodyguard clarified. "He'd like to have a few words with you."

This day was not shaping up well. Reese looked around, but the ambassador was nowhere to be seen. "Oh? Where is he?"

Wallace was already leading the way to the tower elevators. He looked over his shoulder expectantly until Reese fell into step. "He's waiting for you in Mr. Jenkins's office."

He didn't have time for this. "I've got patients to see."

But it was evident that he wasn't going to be doing that immediately. Pressing the down button, Wallace turned and looked at him, towering over him. "He wants to see you now."

Reese sighed. "Now it is."

The statement gave every indication of being a royal summons. That might fly in England and in Spain, but it did very little to impress him, Reese thought. The ambassador might have Jenkins in his pocket, but he had no desire to reside in that small place himself.

By the time he arrived on the first floor and was standing before the chief administrator's door, Reese found that he was in a fairly foul mood.

He was beginning to understand why London was the way she was.

But when he walked into Jenkins's office, which

he found devoid of the chief administrator, Reese was treated to the sight of a smiling, genial man who had made his mark upon the world with his wit, his charm and his intelligence.

The ambassador rose the moment he saw Reese and extended his hand to him, one professional man approaching another. "Dr. Bendenetti, I'm afraid we might have gotten off on the wrong foot."

That, Reese thought, undoubtedly displayed the ambassador's gift for understatement.

Still, he felt it only polite to demur. "That only counts when you're dancing, or in a three-legged sack race at the county fair."

The ambassador laughed. Reese noted that the man's eyes were smiling.

"I've heard some excellent things about you. I believe in doing my homework," the ambassador added.

Reese inclined his head, taking the statement in stride and waiting for the bomb he felt sure was about to be dropped.

"I won't keep you long," the ambassador promised, "but I thought that perhaps an explanation for my earlier abruptness might be in order."

Reese took the seat that the ambassador indicated, waiting. The man, Reese thought, seemed to make himself far more at home in Jenkins's office than Jenkins ever did.

"You might be wondering about the bodyguard detail," Merriweather began genially.

It was more than a detail, it was a major intrusion.

He'd managed to get Jenkins to send away the other members of the ambassador's entourage, but Wallace and the other two men on his team were a fixture.

"It did raise a question in my mind."

Merriweather folded his long, aristocratic hands before him, his tone confidential and intimate. It was a trick he employed successfully in his negotiations.

"Two years ago, the daughter of the ambassador to Chile was kidnapped." His expression was appropriately somber when he said, "They found her body in a shallow grave three months later. Several other daughters of various ambassadors received threatening letters after that—"

"Did your daughter?" Reese interrupted.

Merriweather was honest with him. He'd already sized Reese up as a man who wouldn't react well to being lied to or misled.

"I don't know. She wouldn't tell me if she did. London is very much her own person." He shook his head. There were so many ways in which she reminded him of Anne. "Perhaps too much so. She grew up early." He allowed himself a half smile. "My late wife, Anne, used to say that London was born old." He looked at Reese. "I'd like to see her get to that state in reality. That's why the bodyguards are posted."

Reese could understand the other man's concern. But he could also see how the situation made London feel. She'd told him that she just wanted to have her own space for a little while. In his opinion, being shadowed and protected could get old very quickly.

"But you can't keep that up indefinitely."

Merriweather didn't quite get the response he was hoping for. "I can while I'm part of the diplomatic corps."

Reese was nothing if not practical. "Have there been any more kidnappings or threats recently?"

Merriweather sensed where he was going with this. Where London had gone when she'd made her appeal to terminate the detail.

Until the other thing had begun.

But there was no reason to share that piece of information with the doctor.

"No, but that's not to say that there won't be. I'm telling you this because I think you deserve an explanation and because I don't want you to become a tool for her to use in eluding the bodyguards, Doctor. Mr. Jenkins told me that you were quite annoyed at having the detail on the floor."

He made no apologies for his actions. "They do get in the way."

"I'm willing to pay to compensate for any inconvenience that it might cause you or the hospital." He took out his checkbook to show he was serious and tossed it on the desk beside him. "My daughter is very precious to me."

Reese didn't care for the implication—that his cooperation could be bought. "You might try telling her that."

The ambassador's eyes narrowed. He had the sensation of butting heads with a ram. He was accustomed to being listened to. "I'm quite capable of conducting my own private affairs."

"I'm sure you are," Reese said politely. He rose to his feet. "I have patients to see, Ambassador. So, if there is nothing else—"

Merriweather stood up as well. His look pinned Reese to the wall. "Stay on my side, Dr. Bendenetti and you won't be sorry."

It was a threat, uttered in a silken voice, placed on a silver tray. But it was a threat nonetheless. "I don't take sides, Ambassador. All I do is try to make my patients well."

With that, he left the office. On his way out, he passed a worried-looking Jenkins, who was out in the hall looking like a displaced person.

"Don't worry, Seymour, your contributions are still all safe," was all Reese said as he kept on walking.

He heard a relieved sigh in his wake.

Chapter 7

Passing the nurses' station, Reese walked toward London's suite.

The chair outside the door was vacant. Absently he wondered where the man who was usually posted outside her door had gone.

According to the head nurse, there were three bodyguards in all, and they worked in shifts. Pleasant enough, they tried to remain as unobtrusive as three six-foot-plus linebackers could be.

But this linebacker was missing. Reese smiled to himself as he entered the suite. Grant was probably going to have the other man's head when he heard the bodyguard was "missing" from his post.

The first thing Reese noticed were the two suitcases packed and ready by the door. The lady didn't travel lightly, even to the hospital. He'd seen Grant carrying in various items that had been deemed indispensable during the past seven days. Somehow he figured there'd be more to pack.

London sat perched on her bed, looking lovelier than should have been legally allowed.

Crossing to her, Reese remembered to pick up the chart. He didn't remember to flip it open. Instead he just stood for a moment, looking at her.

When she turned toward him, Reese finally found his tongue.

"Big day today."

He noticed she was wearing high heels and stockings. And a snug, light-blue skirt.

"Yes, I get 'sprung.'"

"You could have left two days ago," he reminded her. He'd offered then to discharge her early because of the rapid progress she'd made over the course of the past four days. Had she been a patient on one of the lower floors with the usual medical coverage, London would have been sent home within three or four days at the most. Beds were needed and insurance only went so far. Unless there was a major reversal in the patient's recovery, they didn't stay long in the hospital no matter what kind of surgery they had.

But above the drone of the common and the ordinary was the world of the privileged, the world whose populace could afford these inordinately expensive hospital suites without blinking an eye.

The final bill in this case was to be sent to London's father at his insistence. He'd left instructions with the chief hospital administrator that his daughter was to remain in the hospital suite for as long as it was thought necessary and until she was truly ready to go home. Since there was currently only one other patient on the tower floor, a film star, the hospital administration was not in a hurry to release London if she chose to remain.

She chose to remain.

The fact that she did made Reese wonder, considering what she'd told him previously about her feelings regarding hospitals.

"I wanted to be sure I was well enough to be on my own—" She thought of Wallace and Kelly and Andrews, the two other bodyguards. On her own. Now there was a joke. She was never really alone, not anymore. "In a manner of speaking."

"I thought you said you hated hospitals."

"I do." She looked around the large room. The rug here was more plush than that found in the rest of the hospital, and the walls had been done with Wedgwood-blue-and-white wallpaper. "This was more like being in a resort. Without the cabana boys," she added, a smile curving her lips as she raised her eyes to his.

He took her pulse in self-preservation, then went on to measure her blood pressure. It gave his hands something to do, as well as something to occupy his mind. He didn't like where it was going of its own volition.

Finished, he remembered to make the notations on

her chart, then flipped the cover closed. He handed her a pink piece of paper he'd just finished signing.

"A pink slip?" Her smile widened, becoming positively dazzling as she turned the paper around in her hand, studying it. "Are you firing me, *Dr.* Bendenetti?"

She was still emphasizing his title, as if somehow it was a private joke between the two of them. Except that he wasn't exactly sure what they were laughing at. "From the hospital, yes." He tapped the paper. "Those are your discharge orders."

London placed the slip on top of the purse she'd had Wallace bring her from her apartment. "Kind of like a 'get out of jail' card in Monopoly." She made her way over to Reese until they were standing within a breath of each other. Or closer.

"If you like." He inclined his head. "Now, I want you—" He faltered a moment as he realized just how close he and London were actually standing.

She turned her face up to his, encouragement in her eyes. She liked the way that phrase sounded, all by itself, without any adornments. He wanted her. "Yes?"

If she were standing any closer to him, she would have had to take up residency in his lab pocket. And her breathy question brought home to him what he was wrestling with. He did want her. There was no sense in lying to himself.

Every visit to her room at the hospital, no matter how much he tried to keep a tight rein on his thoughts, made him acutely aware of that desire.

Had they met under different circumstances, London Merriweather might just have been the woman to cause him to find that small island of time that wasn't taken up by patients, responsibilities and duties and then share it with her.

To what end? he demanded silently.

London represented the top of Mt. Everest, and he was just one of the low-lying villages at the base of the peak. They had nothing in common other than existing on the same planet, in the same hemisphere.

He was lucky he couldn't start anything that promised only to end disastrously.

Clearing his throat, he tried to clear his thoughts at the same time. "I want you to come see me in my office in a week."

Her eyes held his. "You want to let a whole week go by?"

They were having two very different conversations here, using the same words. Even in a simple skirt and blouse, she made a tempting seductress, he thought. He was willing to bet that she was a force to be reckoned with at an embassy ball.

He laughed at himself silently. The only kind of ball he was acquainted with was the kind that periodically went by home plate. Their worlds were as different as different could be.

Reese did his best to maintain the boundaries he knew were proper. "That is the customary length of time between discharge and follow-up visit in this kind of case. Of course, if you experience any pain or have any of these symptoms—" he handed her a list of the various things she needed to watch out for and be aware of ''—don't hesitate to call me right away.''

Taking the paper he gave her, London folded it slowly and then tucked it into her purse. Her eyes remained on him the entire time. A smile curved her mouth. ''I'll be sure to do that.''

''Otherwise, call my office to arrange for an appointment.'' As an afterthought, he reached into his shirt pocket beneath the lab coat and took out one of his cards, then handed that to her, as well.

His duty done, he knew he should be leaving. Glancing toward the door, he lingered. ''Your father coming by to take you home?''

She shook her head. There had been no long visit, no clearing of the air between them the way she always secretly hoped there might be. Try as she might not to be disappointed when it didn't come about, she always was and called herself a fool because of it.

''Dad's back in Madrid, making the world safe for flamenco music.'' And then, hearing her own words, London flushed. He was an outsider, a stranger, he shouldn't be subjected to the civilized feud that was being waged between her and her father. ''I'm sorry, did that sound very bitter?''

There was something soft about her, something vulnerable when she apologized. Even offhandedly, the way she did now.

''Maybe not bitter,'' he allowed generously, ''but pretty sarcastic.''

He was letting her off easy. Another yes man? No,

she didn't think so. Unless she was mistaken, Dr. Reese Bendenetti was his own man and no one else's. It might be mildly interesting to dawdle with him for a while.

His mouth had been tempting her ever since she could focus her eyes.

"I don't know what I expected," she admitted honestly. "You'd think at my age it wouldn't matter anymore. Parental bonding," she added, when she realized that she was rambling.

There was sympathy in his eyes. That threw her. "It matters at any age. For what it's worth, he told me that you were very precious to him."

She looked at him in surprise. That didn't sound like Mason Merriweather. "You didn't strike me as the kind of man who lied."

"I don't."

Everyone lied, she thought. Everyone said things they didn't mean to get things they wanted. Men said they loved you just to get you into their beds. But she was immune to all that because she was prepared for lies, expected lies.

But this great big medicine man seemed almost unshakably honest.

It was a great facade, she thought. "Not even little white lies to help patients along?"

He actually considered the question for a moment. "Maybe if you had two minutes to live, I might let you think you had more by not putting a number on it, but as far as I'm concerned, lies do a disservice to the liar and the li-ee."

"Li-ee?" she echoed, laughing.

Her eyes sparkled when she laughed like that. It made her look softer. Not quite the girl next door—he doubted if anything could transform her into that—but definitely softer. "Sometimes there isn't a word to fit the occasion, so I make one up."

"A surgeon and a lexicographer, very impressive." Amusement highlighted her features as she studied his face. "What else can you do, *Dr.* Bendenetti?"

"My rounds."

Reese began to back away—before he couldn't. He had an uneasy feeling that if he didn't put some space between himself and London, there wouldn't be any in a few minutes. Because more than anything else he wanted to kiss this woman who was sorely tempting him and threatening everything he'd always believed in, every rule he'd ever set down for himself.

He paused right before the door. "You'll be all right? There's someone to take you home?"

The amusement didn't abate. It made him wonder if she was able to read his mind. Probably. Very savvy ladies could do anything they set their minds to.

"Two very different questions, *Dr. Bendenetti.* But to answer your last question first, yes, there's someone to take me home. As for my being all right..." She shrugged philosophically. *"Que sera, sera."*

She'd hit upon one of his mother's favorite songs, and a saying she quoted often enough to become a family logo on their coat of arms, if they had such a thing. "That only worked for Doris Day in *The Man Who Knew Too Much.*"

She was clearly impressed. "Wait, you didn't tell me you were a film buff—"

Hungry for anything American while being shuttled from one country to another when she was a child, and then during her long stay at the boarding school in Switzerland, London had watched any old American movie she could find.

"I'm not," he confessed. "My mother is. She liked to keep the television set on at all times whenever she was home. I kind of absorbed a great deal of the trivia by osmosis." It was time to leave. He couldn't allow himself to be distracted any longer. "No more racing, London," he warned as he began to open the door. And then he added one final instruction. "Be good to yourself."

"Maybe I need someone to show me how."

When he turned around to look at her before leaving, there was that same flippant smile on her face, but her eyes, her eyes didn't have that know-it-all look. They weren't flippant. There was something in them, a sadness that spoke to him for an instant.

And then it was gone.

She hadn't meant to get so serious. It was just that, during off-guard moments, there was something about this doctor who had saved her. Something she couldn't put her finger on. In an odd way, whenever he entered the room, he made her feel safe, as if everything was going to be all right. As if he was going to take care of her.

As if.

She knew it was ridiculous to feel that way. Outside of the follow-up visit, she'd probably never see him again. They clearly existed in two very different worlds. Unless she became involved in some kind of a fund-raiser for the hospital, there wasn't a chance in hell that they would stumble across each other again.

Besides, London reminded herself abruptly, she'd made a career of not getting involved with anyone. That included men with soulful eyes, an easy smile and a bedside manner that made it almost worthwhile being in an accident. You never knew when the next abandonment was waiting for you, and she for one wasn't going to be caught by surprise ever again.

Not ever.

There it was again, that electricity. He could feel it crackling all the way from across the room. Trying to console himself that it was only extreme static electricity, nothing more, he nodded toward the door he held ajar. ''Should I send in your bodyguard?''

She would rather have him take her home, but she'd laid enough groundwork today. Being overly pushy wasn't her style. She lifted her shoulders and then let them drop carelessly. It was time to get back to business as usual.

''Might as well.''

Reese didn't even have to look around when he opened the door. Wallace had reappeared and was taking up all the available space in the doorway. Because of the hour, the man's appearance on the scene surprised him. "I thought Kelly had this shift."

"You've been paying attention, Doc," Wallace approved with a mild smile. "Ms. Merriweather's more comfortable with me, so I volunteered to be the one to take her back home."

Made sense. Maybe. Despite the fact that she'd tried to get away from him, she and this hulk were really friends in a strange sort of way. Wallace seemed to be less on London's level than even he was.

Reese took the opportunity to ask the man to verify something for him. "She said her father was back in Madrid."

Wallace was impatient to get back to his charge, but he nodded. "Left three days ago. Why? Is there something you have to tell him?" He didn't add that he wanted to know if it was about London. If it was, he'd find out soon enough.

This was none of his business, Reese told himself. He wasn't supposed to be getting involved in a patient's private life. This wasn't an underage child in a dangerous home situation, so he had no right to ask anything. He shook his head.

"No."

Wallace's natural tendency toward suspicion raised its head. He regarded the surgeon closely. "Then why the question? You'd do better to remember to keep this on a professional level, Doc."

Wallace's constant vigilance was beginning to really annoy him. "Aren't you overstepping your bounds?"

Wallace didn't see it that way. "The bottom line is that I protect Ms. Merriweather. From anything," he added significantly.

He couldn't see London putting up with this kind of thing for very long, and he was surprised she hadn't really rebelled before.

"Gotta take the cotton batting off sometime, 'Daddy,'" Reese informed the other man as he walked away.

He was beginning to experience a great deal of sympathy for London. The phrase "poor little rich girl" was starting to take on new meaning.

"So, how's life with the tower set?" Lukas Graywolf asked when Reese ran into him a few minutes later on the fifth floor of the hospital, commonly thought of as the surgical floor. Reese was back making his rounds, looking in on the three patients on whom he had operated earlier in the week. All three, two men and a teenage girl, had come in after London.

Unlike his ancestors, Lukas enjoyed beating around the bush a little. Right now Reese was really not in the mood for it. "If you're asking about the ambassador's daughter, I just discharged her."

Lukas fell into step with him. He had just come from the cardiac floor and had stopped to look in on a friend who'd had surgery forty-eight hours ago. "So you're down here with the rest of us peasants?"

"Just where I belong," Reese pointed out. And

then he sobered slightly. "That trip of yours to the reservation still on for next month?"

Lukas, a full-blooded Navajo, was the first of his family to go to college, much less medical school. To placate his mother, he didn't practice on the reservation. To placate his conscience, he returned whenever he could with other doctors in tow, all volunteering their time.

Lukas nodded. "My mother says that by the time we get there, we'll be seeing every living, breathing person on the reservation. Word travels faster there than any other place I've ever been to."

Reese remembered the last time they'd gone. It had been a grueling three days during which he hardly remembered sleeping. But the feeling of satisfaction had been overwhelming. "I guess I'd better stock up on some extra candy bars to keep going."

Lukas slanted him a disparaging look. "There'll be hot food, like always."

As he recalled, Lukas's mother was one fine cook. Thinking of the man's mother turned Reese's thoughts immediately toward the newest development in his friend's life. His engagement to an FBI special agent.

Talk about different worlds, he mused, this one took the prize. And yet it seemed to be working. He'd never seen Lukas happier.

"What's the almost Mrs. Graywolf going to be doing while you're gone?" he wanted to know as he stopped by the nurses' station.

"She's taking some vacation time and coming with

us to help.'' It was her generosity of spirit that made him love her as he did. That and the fact that she moved him the way no other woman ever had. ''And to meet my mother. She's already met my uncle,'' he reminded Reese.

Meeting a mother came under the heading of heavy-duty stuff and could definitely weigh in as an entertainment bonus. For the first time that day Reese grinned. ''This promises to be interesting.''

''That's one way to put it.'' Lukas hesitated, then confided his greatest worry, ''My mother always wanted me to marry a girl from our tribe.''

That wasn't unusual, Reese thought. Several of his friends had parents who wanted their children to marry people of like heritage. That sort of thing had been going on since the beginning of time.

''Mothers are like that.'' He picked up three charts from the desk and began to head to the first room. Mr. Walker and his gall bladder.

Lukas glanced at him. ''Your mother wants you to marry a girl from your tribe, too?''

His mother, bless her, was the exception to every rule, save one. ''My mother would be satisfied if I just found someone from my species. She wants grandchildren.''

Lukas was already planning on a family. Girls who looked like the woman who had won his heart. ''Give her some.''

Reese paused in front of Sidney Walker's room. He had no idea why, but he felt a flicker of irritation.

"They skip something in your training? I'm missing one important ingredient. A wife. Or at the very least, a significant other." The fact that he would definitely marry the mother of his child if that ever came to pass was something he felt he could keep to himself.

Lukas saw no problem with that. "Shouldn't be hard for a dedicated young surgeon like you to find himself a wife. Word has it that the ambassador's daughter has eyes for you." He'd seen her being transferred from the ICU to the tower suite. "And she certainly is a looker."

Reese shook his head. "I've never seen it fail. Get a guy ready to walk up the aisle and suddenly he starts trying to get his friends to do the same thing."

Lukas's expression sobered and he shook his head. "Not true."

"No?"

"No," the taller man said firmly, then deadpanned, "Since when are you my friend?"

Reese merely laughed and shook his head, his hand on the swinging door. Mr. Walker had waited long enough. The man was itching to be sent home. "Get back to me when you have exact dates."

"The same goes for you."

One foot in the doorway, Reese paused again. "Come again?"

"With that Merriweather woman."

Lukas of all people didn't need to be told this. "She's a patient, Graywolf."

"You just discharged her," his friend reminded him. "One visit and you're home free."

Reese said nothing as he went to look in on his next patient.

But his friend's words accompanied Reese for the remainder of the day, buzzing around his head like annoying summer flies. They followed him home, as well, at the end of the grueling day.

And it bothered him.

Bothered him a great deal that his thoughts kept returning to London at the oddest moments.

He had no business thinking about her except as a patient who had made an amazingly fast recovery. There'd been nothing to learn from her case, no nugget to squirrel away for a time when he had another patient in her condition.

Outside of the fact that her recovery was swift, there was nothing remarkable about her case.

Other than the woman herself.

Chapter 8

She saw them the instant she stepped off the elevator. They were waiting for her.

Flowers.

Roses from an unknown sender. Big, plump ones that the doorman had brought up to her apartment and placed before the door in her absence.

They were always the same. White roses with an unsigned card.

This one read: "Welcome home. Remember to be careful. Someone loves you."

Reading the words created a chill that wrapped itself around her spine, shimmying up and down. London tried to tell herself that the roses could just as easily have come from one of her friends or from one of the myriad people she'd met during her travels both alone and as part of her father's entourage. After all, her hospital room had been filled with flowers. Her work had her interacting with a great number of people.

The flowers and note could have come from anyone of them.

They could have, but they didn't. Because anyone else would have signed the note, and this one was unsigned. Just as the other five had been.

Her heart had almost stopped when she'd first seen the roses sitting there before her door, artfully arranged in a lovely blue crystal vase, the florist's logo on the side of the envelope. Blue, because that was her favorite color.

Whoever was sending them had done his homework.

Seeing the vase, Wallace had cursed under his breath. One of the things London liked about him was that he never said anything offensive loudly. He'd started to pick up the flowers—vase, card and all—ready to throw them away.

But she had stopped him, hoping against hope that she was wrong. That the color of the roses was just a coincidence. She held her hand out for the small envelope. "No, I want to see it."

Wallace's expression had registered his doubt over the wisdom of her request. "Ms. London—"

She could tell by his tone that he was trying to change her mind, but he never argued, never tried to browbeat her the way her father did. That, too, was in his favor.

"It might be from a friend," she pointed out.

"Maybe the wrong kind of friend," was all he said politely. He watched her face for a reaction as she opened the card, ready to take his cue.

He saw the brief moment of fear in her eyes and his heart ached.

She slipped the note back into the envelope. "I still think it might just be someone who's painfully shy. Not everyone who's persistent is a stalker."

But even as she said it, she was beginning to believe in her own explanation less and less. The roses and unsigned notes had begun arriving six weeks ago, strategically placed where she would just happen upon them. At first it was a single rose, then two, three, swiftly blossoming into a bouquet. The vase before her held two dozen.

Ironically, the first rose and note had arrived just as she had almost convinced her father that there was no need for the bodyguard detail that had been following her around like a string of discarded dental floss that had somehow attached itself to the heel of her shoe. But when Wallace called the ambassador and told him about the rose and the card on the doorstep, any hope she had of being rid of her bodyguards was terminated. The ambassador wouldn't hear of it.

Wallace put out his hand. He made her think of a gentle, trained bear.

"Give me the card," he requested. "I'll see if the florist can describe whoever sent the roses." He held the card through his handkerchief. "If he wrote the card, there'll be fingerprints."

She smiled. Good old Wallace. He never gave up,

even when it was hopeless. They both knew that there was a pattern being followed. There would be no identification, no prints other than those belonging to the florist or one of his or her assistants.

"That's what you always say, and it always turns out that someone has phoned the order in using some-one's else's credit card and that person always turns out to be surprised because they never heard of the florist." She told herself to enjoy the flowers and for-get the implications. Wallace wouldn't let anything happen to her, and who knew, maybe whoever was sending them was content with things the way they were. "Face it, my secret admirer's got this thing down pat."

The wide shoulders rose and fell. "Everybody slips up eventually."

"Everybody?" she echoed, a smile curving her mouth. "Even you?"

Wallace returned her smile, suddenly looking like a young boy instead of the seasoned professional he was.

"Almost everyone." He nodded at the flowers. "Want me to toss them out?"

"Oh no, Wallace, why take it out on them? They're beautiful. Whoever this secret admirer is," she re-fused to label him anything else, even in her mind, "he's got good taste."

Wallace looked at her. "He'd have to, Ms. London. He picked you."

Then, before she could make a response, Wallace

unlocked the door for her and turned away to pick up her luggage.

She could have sworn she'd seen him blush.

The man was a positive dear, she thought, crossing her threshold, and she felt guilty about making his job difficult. She just wished that it didn't conflict with her own sense of freedom.

For now she was just going to enjoy being back in her own apartment and not think about anything else.

Except maybe, she thought with a smile as she sank down on her sofa and kicked off her shoes, a very sexy surgeon who did a great deal to get her blood moving.

She sighed with contentment as Wallace placed the vase on top of her baby grand.

Keeping perpetually busy, Reese had not allowed himself to realize how much he missed seeing London until he walked into examining room number three and saw her sitting on the examining table, waiting for him, her legs dangling over the side.

She looked like an innocent and a temptress all rolled into one.

She looked up when he opened the door. Her eyes met his instantly, taking him prisoner. Reese had to remind himself of the boundaries that still existed, though it wasn't easy.

But then, she wasn't the kind of woman who made things easy on a man.

She just made him glad to be alive.

He'd picked up her chart from the see-through

holder on the outside of the door where his nurse had left it. Reese flipped it open now, forcing himself to concentrate on the reason London was here.

Quickly he scanned the few notes that his nurse had made. Everything seemed to be in order.

Closing the folder, he placed it on the counter and looked at London. "So how have you been feeling? Since there haven't been any emergency phone calls, I take it your amazing progress has continued."

She'd been tempted to call him. More than once. But there'd been no reason other than she wanted to hear his deep, masculine voice. She had no symptoms to report, no flare-ups. London indulged in games on occasion, but she didn't believe in outright lies. She supposed that did give them something in common.

"That's me," she affirmed blithely. "Wonder Woman. Or is that Superwoman?"

As far as he was concerned, she was a woman in a class all by herself. "I don't think you need a secret identity. Or me, for that matter." Taking her chin gently in his hand, he turned her head so that he could look at her left temple. Even that minor contact between them sent unsettling ripples undulating through him. "The cut is healing nicely, and the bruise seems to be going away."

She could feel her heart speeding up. The sensation intrigued her. She didn't normally react this way to something so innocent. After all, he was just examining her, not seducing her.

"A little makeup doesn't hurt," she finally managed to say.

Reese gently rubbed his thumb along her temple to see if any telltale powder or cream came off. When he looked, there was nothing on his thumb. But a great deal was going on inside of him.

"No," he replied quietly, his eyes on hers, "no makeup. That's just your body at work, taking care of you." He continued holding her chin for another long moment. Wondering what it would be like to kiss her.

Her nerves felt as if they were tiny beads of water on a hot skillet, bouncing here and there. It took skill to mask her reaction. "Dr. Bendenetti?"

"Yes?"

She smiled then, her temple moving ever so slightly against his fingers. Like a playful kitten rubbing against the hand of someone who was petting it. "Are you through with my face yet?"

He sincerely doubted that he would ever be through with her face. It was the kind of face that haunted a man, the kind that wasn't easily forgotten.

Reese dropped his hand, self-conscious, though he tried not to show it. "You can have it back."

"My ears thank you," she quipped. The smile that rose to her lips was nothing short of wicked. And stimulating. "So, do you want me to disrobe?"

Oh, yes.

The silent response bursting across his brain left him thunderstruck. He'd seen her nude during the operation, when sections of her body had been left uncovered so that he could work. When they'd thrown a fresh sheet over her, there'd been a split second

when her undraped body had been exposed. Even
with the bandages and the peril of a life-and-death
situation, it had registered in the recesses of his mind
as damn near perfect.

But that had been a passing, neutral observation.
Her suggestion now brought an entirely different response coursing through his veins. Reminding him
that he didn't get out very much.

He shook his head, taking a step back from the
examination table.

"Won't be necessary. Just lift up your sweater so
that I can see how your ribs are healing."

When she raised the left side of her sweater, a pot-
pourri of colors met his eye. Yellow, purple, blue. But
none of the colors were as bold as they had been
several days after she'd been brought in.

He allowed himself a smile. "Looks like you have
a pretty good rainbow going there."

She looked down to the area under scrutiny, acutely
aware of his nearness. He was wearing a cologne she
was familiar with and liked. It was arousing.

"All the basic colors," she agreed. It still hurt
when she shifted, but not nearly as much as it had
before. "And a few not so basic."

Gingerly, Reese touched the area all around the
bruises. "Does this hurt?"

The ache she was experiencing intrigued her. It had
very little to do with the fact that after two weeks,
she was still somewhat sore to the touch and everything to do with the doctor who was touching her.
London caught her breath as something hot and de-

manding zipped through her with an urgency she was unfamiliar with.

"A little," she breathed.

Very gently, Reese dropped the sweater back into place. "That'll pass before you know it. Everything seems to be in order." A smile came into his eyes as he raised his gaze to her face. "Perfect, actually."

Shifting on the table, London adjusted her sweater slightly and looked at him. "So I don't need to come back?"

He was really trying to maintain the lines that were drawn between them—and getting no help from her. "Not unless you start experiencing any of those symptoms on the list I gave you."

She nodded, as if taking everything in slowly. "So, you're discharging me."

"Yes."

"We're no longer doctor-patient." It wasn't so much a question as it was an establishment of the new parameters that existed between them.

He allowed himself a slight smile. "Well, I'm still a doctor, just not yours." He decided to qualify that. "Unless you need me."

She took it one step further. "What if I need you, but not as a doctor?"

Saying nothing, he waited for her to elaborate.

"What if I need someone to talk to? Someone who isn't part of my usual insane existence." She wasn't sure why, but for some reason she didn't completely fathom, she found herself trusting this man, knowing that at least when it came to keeping confidences, she could rely on him. As for the rest, well, she wasn't going to think about that. She wasn't looking for anything permanent anyway. Quite the opposite. "Could I pick up the phone and call you?" she pressed. "Just to talk?"

He was desperately trying to continue thinking like a doctor, but she was making it very hard for him to maintain his boundaries. But then, he *was* discharging her from his care.

He made one last notation on her chart and closed it with finality before looking at her. "If you can reach me."

"I thought doctors could always be reached." She looked significantly at the pager at his waist, then raised her eyes again to his.

There was no doubt about it, the man definitely intrigued her. She'd given him every possible opening, and he hadn't attempted to pursue her, hadn't even remotely attempted to take advantage of the situation, even at the hospital when she had all but poured herself against his side when he'd taken her for a walk down the hallway. Granted she'd been weak, but that didn't change the fact that he hadn't even tried to press her closer to his side. The man was chivalry personified.

Men had always come on to her, ever since she'd reached puberty and suddenly transformed from a mildly pretty little girl into a child-woman in possession of a woman's body. She'd always had more attention than she'd wanted.

Yet this man was restrained by things like ethics

and integrity even while he attracted her with such force that she found her teeth being jarred.

Breaking down his reserves seemed like the perfect challenge to her.

"We can," he agreed. "For medical reasons."

Without making a move, she seemed to draw closer to him as she asked, "How about for other reasons?"

He laughed, shaking his head. The woman was definitely one of a kind. "Have you always been a shrinking violet?"

London tossed her hair over her shoulder, her manner just the slightest bit defensive, even though she told herself there was no need to be. She was what she was. "Shrinking violets get stepped on, *Dr.* Bendenetti. I don't intend to be stepped on."

He wondered if anyone actually had, once upon a time, stepped on her, and that was why she came across as she did. "I think, under the circumstances, you can start calling me Reese now."

He watched the smile unfold in her eyes first, slipping down to her lips, curving them appealingly. "Does this mean I made the cut?"

She'd lost him. "Excuse me?"

Very slowly she slipped off the table in one long, languid movement, never taking her eyes off his. "From patient to friend?"

He looked at her for a long moment. He knew only one way of dealing with people, be they patients or just the people he came in contact with, and that was honestly. "I don't toss the term around loosely. Being friends means something to me."

He meant that, she realized. Her smile this time was not for show. It came from somewhere deep within. "I certainly hope so."

She used her looks to attract, her humor as a defense, he noted, and found himself being intrigued by her as much as he was attracted to her.

That caused him to step out on the limb he'd known all along was waiting for him.

"Would you like to go out to dinner tonight?" He tried to recall his appointments. There were only two patients to see at Blair Memorial. "My rounds at the hospital shouldn't take me too long."

From out of nowhere a little voice exclaimed, *Yes!* as she did her best to remain casual. "Would you like to pick me up at my place, or would you rather that I met you somewhere?"

A thoroughly modern woman, Reese thought. Although he admired that, there was a part of him that still enjoyed the old-fashioned roles that had once been assigned to men and women.

"I'll pick you up." Taking her folder with him, he began to cross to the door. There was another patient waiting for him in the next room. "Eight o'clock all right?"

Her eyes crinkled as anticipation took another pass through her. She marveled at the new sensation. "Eight is perfect."

He hesitated at the door, remembering her hulking shadow. Would Grant be coming along with them, or content to post himself outside the restaurant?

"By the way, should I make the reservation for two or three?"

London laughed, understanding perfectly. "Wallace is about to get the night off."

There was no room for argument in her tone, but Reese still had his doubts. The other man seemed to take his job exceedingly seriously. "Can you dismiss him that easily?"

If either Andrews or Kelly were scheduled to be on duty, London knew she wouldn't have to think twice about her answer. The other two bodyguards took their orders from Wallace, but she had discovered that she could twist them around her finger when she needed to. However, Wallace was the one on evening duty and twisting him was another matter.

He wasn't as easily led around as the other two. But, on the plus side, there hadn't been any flowers on her doorstep or notes in the mail since the ones that arrived the day she'd returned from the hospital. With any luck Wallace was beginning to relax and could be convinced to see things her way at least for a few hours. She wanted to spend the evening with the good doctor without the sensation that someone was looking over her shoulder, observing her every move.

"I can appeal to his sense of fair play." If she really put her heart into it, she felt certain she could get Wallace to listen to her. After all, it was only for one evening and it wasn't as if she and Reese were going to a deserted beach. "You look like you can take care of yourself," she observed. "I can tell him that I'll have you to protect me from being whisked off by third-world terrorists or ninja warriors.''

Her flippant choice of culprits aroused his curiosity. Was the truth in there somewhere? ''Is that who kidnapped the Chilean ambassador's daughter?''

The question caught her off guard. But only for a moment. ''So, you know about that. Who told you? Wallace?''

''Your father.''

That shouldn't have surprised her. It was her father's method of getting his way. She'd heard that there'd been a power struggle between the two men as to whether the entourage would remain on the hospital floor.

She nodded. ''Terrorist, they think. But there haven't been any incidents or kidnapping threats in eighteen months.''

If that was the case, then why was the ambassador spending good money to keep three bodyguards looking after her around the clock? ''So why keep the detail in place?''

She shrugged. ''He's being overly cautious.'' More than that, it was a power thing. ''And it's a way to keep me in place. So he thinks,'' she added with a wink. Straightening her shirt, which had hiked up slightly during her descent from the table, she slipped the chain strap of her purse onto her shoulder. ''So, I'll see you at eight?''

''Eight.'' This time, to assure his exit, he opened the door.

''You have the address?''

"It's in your file," he reminded her, indicating the folder in his hand.

"This is smaller." She opened her purse, took out a card and handed it to him.

There were several numbers on the card, covering home, office, cell phone and fax, plus the word "Fund-raiser" beneath her embossed name. He looked at her in mild surprise. Up to now, he'd thought of her only as the ambassador's daughter. It never occurred to him that she was anything beyond that. That probably would have irked her, he realized.

"You're a fund-raiser?"

"It's a good excuse for throwing parties." She wiggled past him, making her way out of the room first. "I like to party."

He didn't doubt it for a moment, he thought as he watched his ex-patient walk down the hall to the reception desk. The saunter she added to her step was for his benefit, and he enjoyed it as such.

She knew he was looking and he knew that she knew. He figured that put them on an equal footing.

For the first time in a long time, he found himself looking forward to the evening for reasons that went beyond his just crashing on his bed and getting some well-deserved sleep.

Chapter 9

Reese found himself wrestling with conflicting desires all afternoon.

The temptation to pick up the telephone and cancel their dinner date was great. The temptation to see London again was greater.

Which worried him.

Seeing London again shouldn't have mattered. Not in the way that it did. It should have been one of those things he could take in stride routinely. But going out with beautiful women could not, by any stretch of the imagination, be considered as part of his routine. When he saw women at all, they were not at their best: distraught before surgery, pale and recovering afterward. And he'd never gone out with any of his patients, not even after he'd signed off on their care.

This was different. It *felt* different and if pressed,

he couldn't say whether or not he was happy about that.

After leaving the hospital, Reese went home to get dressed. Once he was ready, there was nothing left to do but pick London up at her apartment.

Reese glanced at the pager on his belt and waited for the Fates to intervene. The Fates were sleeping or on vacation. The pager remained silent.

It was either an omen or not. In either case, there was a lovely woman waiting for him on the upscale side of town.

Reese got into his car and drove.

"But I'm giving you the night off, Wallace. Go, have a life."

London had left this clash of wills to the very end, after she'd gotten dressed for the evening. She looked at the man who was giving her such a hard time over her minor request and wondered why she couldn't have been born to someone less ambitious in life. Someone who ran the corner bakery, or worked in insurance. Someone whose life would not have dragged her into the limelight.

Wallace returned her pugnacious look with a patient one. She was dressed simply but elegantly. The lady had style, and it was, he thought, in all likelihood wasted on the man she intended to spend the evening with.

"No disrespect, Ms. London, but I don't answer to you, I answer to the ambassador."

She made a vain attempt to usurp her father's

power, knowing she was doomed to fail but bound to try. "There were times at the embassy when I spoke for 'the ambassador.'"

Wallace smiled, seeing right through her. In the eighteen months that he had been head of the detail, he'd gotten to know the way her mind worked pretty well. It was one of his talents. It was what allowed him, at times, to remain ahead of the game.

"We're not talking about choosing a tablecloth or what kind of silverware to use for a reception, we're talking about your life, Ms. London."

She seized the words and tossed them back at him. "Yes, that's exactly it—*my* life. And, Wallace, once in a while, I'd like to live it."

He wouldn't be budged on this. Not with all the dynamite or perturbed looks in the world.

"That's my whole point, Ms. London. I'm here to make sure you *have* a life and that some jerk doesn't steal it away from you." He smiled reassuringly at her. "I won't get in the way. You won't even know I'm there." She should know this by now, he thought. He might be heavyset, but he was very good at disappearing, at blending in.

She threw up her hands. "How can I not know? You'll be watching." The thought left her unsettled. She liked Wallace, but she didn't like the thought of his watching her every move. Bodyguard or not, there was something creepy about that.

"Not you," he reminded her patiently. They'd been through this before. "Everyone else. At a discreet distance,'' he added though he didn't think, by now, he should have to.

London blew out an exasperated breath, defeat closing in. There was no way around this. Wallace couldn't be cajoled into relenting. The best she could hope for was a compromise. ''A discreet distance?''

Wallace raised his hand as if taking a solemn oath. ''Yes.''

''At all times?'' She didn't want to be eating dessert and suddenly look up to see him standing there.

He made no attempt to drop his hand. ''Yes.''

She cocked her head, watching his eyes. When he tried to hide things, he looked away. ''And if he brings me back to my apartment, where will you be?''

His eyes never left hers. He knew what she was doing and was, again, ahead of the game. It was his job. ''Outside the building, in my car, same place Kelly is every night.''

It was Kelly who was supposed to be on the night shift, but Wallace knew better than to trust the younger man. All London had to do was look at the man and he gave in to her. But for the time being, Kelly suited his purposes, and he wasn't about to terminate him.

London swallowed a sigh. She supposed she couldn't ask for more, not without having Wallace violate some kind of client-employee trust he had going with her father. ''Oh, all right, I give up. But if I see any sign of that crewcut of yours—''

He grinned his small-boy grin at her. ''You can have me replaced.''

She knew the man actually meant what he said. And that he only had her well-being in mind. London put out her hand. "Deal."

His large hand swallowed hers up. His handshake was firm, binding. "Deal."

At exactly eight o'clock London heard the doorbell ring. Habit had her looking at her watch. The man was incredibly punctual, she thought, smoothing down a dress that needed no smoothing.

A seasoned traveler, able to converse and be amusing in no less than three languages beyond her own native tongue, and part of the international scene since before she could remember, London still felt as if several single-engine planes were taking off in her stomach as the sound of the chimes died away.

This was silly. There was no reason to feel unsettled. It had to be some residual posttraumatic stress because of the accident, London told herself.

But there was no denying that her pulse had kicked up a notch as she opened the door.

Reese was wearing a navy-blue sports jacket over a light-blue shirt. He had on gray slacks and looked very much as if he belonged on the cover of *Heartthrob Monthly*. It was the first time she'd seen him without a white lab coat draped over him.

Her eyes smiled as she greeted him. "You clean up nice."

She was wearing a simple black dress. It looked perfect on her.

Funny, he'd never pictured London wearing something as somber as black. But on her, black wasn't somber. She managed to bring life and color to it.

Reese inclined his head. "I could say the same to you."

She batted her lashes at him in an exaggerated fashion. Teasing or not, he still felt a knot forming in his stomach. The kind that would take hours to undo. "Flatterer."

Slipping his hands into his pockets, Reese waited as she picked up her purse. He glanced around the immediate area. There was no one around. Despite her promise, he'd expected to see the bodyguard right behind her.

"Where's your shadow? Don't tell me that you managed to get rid of him." The man didn't strike him as being easily set aside. The lady had to take after her father when it came to a silver tongue.

Draping a silver-fringed shawl about her shoulders, she looked up at Reese. "I'd like to tell you that, but I don't believe in lying on first dates."

The word stood out before him in huge neon lights. Until she'd said it, he hadn't really labeled this evening as such. But that's what it was. A date. A bona fide date. He'd absently thought the term and the custom had gone out of fashion, that men and women were now somehow just thrown together by happenstance.

He thought back to London's accident and decided that maybe he wasn't that far from being right.

Reese assumed her answer meant that the man was coming with them. He looked around again. "Then, where is he? Is he going to jump out from behind a door? Or from the elevator when it opens?''

She walked out of her apartment, locking the door behind her. Turning, she threaded her arm through Reese's. ''Wallace promised to behave himself and keep a 'discreet distance' away from us at all times so he doesn't spoil the evening.''

As long as she was in it, Reese doubted that anything could really spoil the evening.

Pressing for the elevator, Reese thought of telling her that, but then didn't. There was no doubt in his mind that she had enough people flattering her, enough people telling her things she knew they thought she would want to hear, and he didn't want to be lumped in with a crowd like that.

Didn't want to be lumped in with anyone else at all when it came to London. Although he kept telling himself it really shouldn't matter.

It did.

The elevator arrived and they stepped inside. They had it entirely to themselves.

''So, where are we going?'' London wanted to know.

He'd debated over that, as well. There were places in and around Bedford that boasted excellent cuisine, fancy decor and fancier prices, places created for the discerning diner. But unless he missed his guess, she'd been to many places like that, taken there by men who wanted to impress her.

Given that her past dinner companions were probably all in a class he didn't belong to, there was no point in trying to compete with them. He might as well take her to a place where he was comfortable.

"There's this restaurant, Malone's, where I used to go to celebrate while I was in medical school."

She smiled. "I'd like that." She wanted to get to know the man he'd been, as well as the man he was. "Who did you celebrate with when you celebrated?"

If he didn't know better, he would have said she was probing for information. Just small talk, he told himself. "Friends."

Friends. London decided to leave it at that for the time being. It was a nice, neutral term that could mean anything, include any gender.

Maybe he just meant hoisting a few with the boys. She wasn't averse to going to a place like that. A quiet little bar would certainly be a change of pace. Wallace might have a canary, but she was determined to enjoy herself.

Without realizing it, she wrapped her arm a little tighter through Reese's.

She might not have realized it, but Reese did.

The moment they stepped out of the elevator and walked through the lobby, the red-liveried doorman snapped to attention. Tipping his cap, he hurried ahead of London to get to the door and open it. Barely a couple of inches taller than she, the man beamed at her with approval.

"You're looking exceptionally lovely tonight, Ms. Merriweather."

London took the compliment in stride, neither

preening nor looking down at the man. Instead she smiled graciously. "Thank you, John."

"Fan club?" Reese whispered against her ear as they walked through the door the man held open for them.

His breath against the shell of her ear created a downdraft that zipped along her spine. The reaction surprised and delighted her. There was no doubt about it, there was something electric going on between them, and she fully intended to enjoy it.

She turned her face toward him and replied in a soft whisper, "I give generous tips during the holidays and on birthdays."

He'd left his Corvette parked near the entrance. "You know the doorman's birthday?"

"Knowing a little something about the people you come in daily contact with takes away that depersonalizing edge that always exists." A quirky smile curved her lips. "I learned that at my father's knee. Not that he bothered to teach me anything, I just learned by observing."

Reese didn't know if she was covering up something she viewed as making her vulnerable, or if she was espousing a philosophy she believed in. London Merriweather was a puzzle all right. Warm and open one moment, flippant and distant the next.

He couldn't help wondering which London was the real one.

The doorman followed them to where the car was parked and insisted on opening the passenger door for her. He'd used his considerable bulk to block Reese's access to that side.

Reese smiled to himself as he rounded the hood and got in on his side. The lady had admirers in all shapes and sizes.

"Those must be some tips," he murmured.

London settled in, buckling up. She nodded at the doorman as he stepped away. "Actually, I haven't given him one yet. He was hired on after Christmas and his birthday isn't for another month." She waved to the man as Reese pulled away from the curb. "I think he's just new and a little zealous in doing his job."

Reese thought it was a little more than that. He guided his red vehicle into the main flow of traffic. "You seem to make people come alive around you, London. You bring out a zest in them."

"Do I?" She turned the comment around in her head and found it appealing. Twisting in her seat, she looked at him. "How about you, Reese? Do I make you come alive?"

"Me? I'm always this way," he told her, keeping his eyes on the road.

But he was lying.

It hurt him to watch her with another man.

To see the smile on her lips, the laughter in her eyes, and know that it was there for someone else.

He never felt more alive than when she turned that magic toward him.

Nor more bereft than when he saw it directed toward someone else.

But that would change soon. He promised himself that. Promised her that.

Soon.

When that day came, she'd smile only for him, laugh only for him. Dress only for him.

Undress only for him.

His palms grew sweaty and his breath grew short. He willed his control back. His breathing became steadier again.

He thought about that sometimes. Late at night in his room, staring at his mural, he thought of that. Of having her.

Sometimes it made a pain twist in his belly, wanting her.

It didn't matter to him that there'd been others. That she'd loved other men. He didn't care about her past. He cared only about her future. And that it would be with him.

He followed her with his eyes, thinking of the day that he wouldn't have to follow her at all anymore. The day that they would be standing side by side. Together.

Forever.

Soon.

Reese held the door open for her as she walked into the dimly lit restaurant. Malone's was owned by a transplanted Texan who'd brought a little of his former home into the decor of the restaurant he loved so well.

Reese tried to gauge London's reaction and decided that the woman would make a fair poker player. Still, he could make an educated guess at what was crossing her mind. "Not what you expected, is it?"

"No," she admitted, "it isn't." The floor was wooden, with a high polish to it. There was a bar running along one wall that looked as if it came straight out of a John Wayne Western. The thought made her smile. She'd always loved Westerns. "A lot of men try to impress me because of what they think I'm used to."

He still couldn't tell if she was insulted that he'd brought her here, or amused. "What are you used to?"

"Facades." The rich were very attached to their traditions and to what they felt elevated them above the rest of the world. Her eyes shone as she looked around the small restaurant. There was a charm here, an intimacy that reached out to her and made her feel at home. "I like this." She turned toward him. "I like this a lot."

He felt a sense of relief wash over him. He'd taken a chance bringing her here. "Good."

A hostess came and led them to their table. It was a cozy booth nestled off to the side. "Do you still come here to celebrate?"

Taking a menu from the hostess, he set it in front of him. Reese shook his head in response to London's question. "I don't have as much time to do that as I used to."

She looked at him in amazement. "Not as much time as when you were in medical school? Just how busy do they keep you at that hospital?"

Things were hectic in emergency, but there were lulls, as well. And he was only one of several doctors on rotation. "I keep myself busy. Between the hospital, my own practice and the reservation—"

Reese couldn't mean what she thought he meant. "Reservation, as in restaurant?"

He liked the way the light from the candle caressed her face. Making him want to do the same. He kept his hands in his lap.

"As in Native American. Navajo," he added before she could ask.

London's eyes narrowed as she studied his face. His hair was dark, but his eyes were blue. That didn't quite fit the image. "You're not—"

He smiled. Graywolf would get a kick out of this. "No, I'm not."

"Didn't think so. You don't have the cheekbones for it." Although his hair was certainly the right shade, she thought. Blue black, straight and thick. It made her fingers itch.

The food server, a tall, slender college student in his third year as a drama major, came to take their order for drinks. She asked for red wine to go with the steak she already knew she would be ordering, then waited until the waiter was gone.

Leaning her chin on her hand, she looked up at

Reese, finding him more and more intriguing as the minutes passed. "So what are you doing on a reservation if you don't mind my asking?"

That she thought he'd mind her probing told him that she had a healthy respect for privacy. He liked that. Reese couldn't help wondering how much she minded having hers invaded periodically because of the nature of her father's work.

"It's in Arizona. One of the other doctors on staff grew up there. Once or twice a year he goes back to offer free medical care to the members of his tribe. Sort of a payback, you might say. A few of the other doctors began going with him. It's a pretty healthy-size group now." It was almost his favorite time, he thought. That was what doctoring was all about to him, helping those who were in real need.

The waiter returned with their drinks and placed them on the table. London continued looking at Reese. "Very noble of you."

He shifted, uncomfortable at the focus her words brought. He looked down at the menu. "Pretty much everything here is good."

Compliments embarrassed him, she noted. She liked that. So many men she knew loved bragging about their accomplishments and beating their chests like the Neanderthals they claimed to look down on.

But then, she'd already sensed that Reese Bendenetti was different.

She decided to follow his lead. "How are the portions?"

"Large."

The information pleased her. "Good, I have a big appetite."

Reese finally raised his eyes from the menu. If he remembered his facts, she only weighed one-hundred and ten pounds. "Oh, really?"

His tone catching her attention, she looked up and saw the skeptical, amused look in his eyes. "Yes, really. If you don't believe me, just watch."

He could think of far worse assignments. "I intend to." Whether she ate anything or not.

She laughed softly as she took a sip of her wine. Glancing around, she tried to see where Wallace had stationed himself. But true to his word, he was invisible.

Taking another sip of her wine, London began to relax—as much as she could with all her nerve endings standing at attention in reaction to the man sitting opposite her.

Chapter 10

As the tables began to fill up, the noise in the cozy restaurant increased. London found herself leaning further toward Reese in order to be heard.

"You know, it's funny that you'd pick a place like this."

The glow of the single candle nestled in clear glass found her face and made love to it. He could see her eyes sparkling with humor even in the dim light. Humor that was at no one's expense. There was no need to brace himself against a put-down.

"Why?"

A fond smile curved her lips as her thoughts took her back across the years to a time when things were so much simpler, to a time when she felt safe and protected. And loved.

"Because I love Westerns."

Her answer surprised him, and he looked at her. "You don't seem the type."

What type do I seem to you, Reese? Cold, calculating, spoiled rotten? I'm not any of those things, not really.

But all she said was, "Looks can be deceiving." And then, because being here made her smile from within, she elaborated. "When I was a little girl, I hated the kind of life my parents led, moving from one country to another. Half the time, outside of the embassy, I didn't hear a word of English being spoken. Sometimes in the embassy, as well. I was very, very homesick and desperately hungry for something that would remind me of the sights and sounds of home."

He seemed genuinely interested, she thought, not because she was the ambassador's daughter—he'd already proven that meant nothing to him—but because she was a woman he was sharing the evening with. She liked that. A lot.

"I thought of television as the last bastion of Americana, but of course there were only domestic programs on." She laughed at her own naiveté. "Except for the occasional Western that was thrown in. Half the time it was dubbed, too, but there's no mistaking John Wayne and his pals for bullfighters, no mistaking Monument Valley," she named the popular site in Utah where so many Westerns were filmed, "for the Alps. And whenever I did chance upon one in English, I was in seventh heaven. Westerns were my touchstone, my home base." Her eyes swept over the restaurant. From her vantage point she could see a great deal. "In a way, I feel as if I've come home."

He could almost feel her pleasure. A sense of satisfaction that he rarely experienced away from the operating table filled him. If she hated her parents' lifestyle, he was guessing she probably made her feelings known.

"So you rebelled right from the start?"

Nothing could have been further from the truth. In the beginning. And even after her mother died.

"Oh no, I was a good little daughter. Went to classes, learned the necessary languages, did everything I could to make my father proud of me." Because she felt as if he could see right into her, London lowered her gaze to look at the candlelight trapped in her wineglass. "Until I realized that was one of those impossible feats the wicked witch hands out to the heroine in a Grimms' fairy tale. Rather like being told to move the ocean into a pond using a teaspoon." She saw the odd look on his face and guessed correctly. "You never read that one?"

He laughed softly and shook his head. "Must have been one of the stories I missed."

She liked the sound of his laugh. Even soft, it was deep and rich, like black coffee on a cold winter morning. Bracing. "I didn't. I read everything I could get my hands on. It cut into the loneliness."

She'd said too much, London realized abruptly. She was going to have to watch that. There was something about this semistoic man that made him easy to talk to, but she'd never believed in talking too much.

If you weren't careful, you gave pieces of yourself away.

Westerns and loneliness. They didn't jibe with the woman he was looking at. He took a sip of his wine and shook his head.

"I can't see you as being lonely."

There was a reason for that. She'd gone into reconstruction mode and carefully rebuilt herself a piece at a time, taking as models people she admired. People she wanted to be like.

Opening the menu again, she perused it in earnest this time. "That's because I realized one day that no one was going to notice me if I didn't notice myself." She raised her chin ever so slightly as she continued talking. "That's when I decided to grab life with both hands and make the most of it before it was gone for me the way it was for my mother."

So the very independent London Merriweather was actually a product of both of her parents, he thought. Each had influenced her in his or her own way. She was living for both her mother and herself as she thwarted the father she felt had turned his back on her.

Reese found himself wanting to know things about her. About what she'd been like as a child. About what made her laugh, what made her cry. Things that went far beyond the usual kind of relationship he allowed himself to have, that of a doctor looking out for the well-being of his patient.

She wasn't his patient anymore.

He wanted to know.

Making his selection, he closed the menu and looked at her. "Tell me more about the dutiful daughter."

She picked up on the word he'd chosen: *dutiful.* "Why, do you like obedient women?" She hadn't pegged him for a martinet, but you never knew. She'd been wrong before, although not often.

The woman who had heretofore made the largest impression on his life—his mother—was as independent as they came. If he were ever to seek a wife, that would be the first quality he'd look for. A woman who could stand on her own. Who was soft but not weak.

He caught himself thinking that his mother might like London, and vice versa. "No, I'm just having a hard time envisioning you as someone who ever played by the rules."

She wasn't that much of a rebel, she thought, although she liked the way he was looking at her when he said it. What she didn't like was being boxed in. "Well, I did, for the most part. I let myself be sent away to boarding school—"

He vaguely remembered she'd mentioned that to him before. "How old were you?"

"Eight." It was the last time she allowed herself to be vulnerable, to need someone. Because she had and she'd been ignored. When she had needed comfort the most, her father had turned away from her, leaving her in the care of strangers. It was a slap in the face that had taught her to be self-reliant and never to need anyone.

"Eight," he repeated. "There wasn't much you could do about it."

That was where he was wrong. Even at eight she'd been her mother's daughter. Headstrong even though she was vulnerable. Headstrong *because* she was vulnerable. "I thought about running away. And then, briefly, I thought that if I did what he wanted, if I went away to that Swiss boarding school, my father would miss me and come after me."

The smile on her lips was meant to be flippant, but there was a touch of ruefulness to it. And hurt. Reese could see it, even in the dim light.

"He didn't, of course." She curved her fingers around the glass. "He was relieved not to have to deal with me."

Reese thought her description was probably a little harsh. "I don't think—"

London cut him off. "You don't have to. I was there. I know." Her voice throbbed with emotion. London forced herself to get it under control. "My mother was the only person who truly meant anything to him. With her gone, my father threw himself into the only love he had left, the diplomatic service." Why was she talking about this? The conversation had gotten so deep so quickly. She scrambled for neutral ground. "To his credit, he is very good at it. My father bought his way into his first ambassadorship with hefty campaign donations—it's one of those open secrets no one speaks about in Washington— and turned out to have a natural flare for it. My father gets along with everyone in the world—but me."

She flashed a smile at him that went straight to Reese's gut and threatened the tranquil state of the food he was consuming.

He had to remind himself to breathe. "Did you stay at the boarding school year-round?"

She was as honest with him as she had been with herself of late. "He would have liked that, but the school closed for the summer and during the holidays, so I was brought home, and when I was old enough and presentable enough, he had me playing hostess whenever he threw an embassy ball—they were never parties, always balls, always stately."

She'd tried hard during that time, trying to cull her father's favor by being the perfect little hostess. She'd always been ahead of her years that way. But all she ever received was silence, not approval, and eventually she played the part for herself, not for him.

She shrugged casually. "I didn't mind, I liked dressing up. And my father was generous with his money—why not? He has truckloads of it, parting with some to make his daughter appear attractive so that he could look better to the people he was dealing with presented no hardship."

Looking at her, Reese hardly thought that she would have needed anything beyond the light in her eyes to make her attractive, but he kept the speculation to himself.

"It's where I learned to network," she continued. "So it wasn't a total loss. I discovered that people didn't mind parting with money when they were well fed, entertained and feeling just this side of tipsy."

She smiled, looking at her own glass of wine. "Fundraising for charities seemed a natural jumping-off place for me." Taking the bottle he topped off her glass. She twirled the stem in her fingers. "So, now you have my life story, what's yours?"

He didn't like talking about himself. "It's not very interesting."

Oh no, turnabout was fair play. "I'll be the judge of that. Interest is in the ear of the listener." The din around them was getting overwhelming. London leaned farther forward. "What made you want to become a doctor? It wasn't the money."

She said it as if she knew it for a fact. Her statement stirred his curiosity. "What makes you say that?"

She'd ordered prime rib and took a moment now to savor a bite. It all but melted on her tongue. "If it was the money, you wouldn't be going off to the reservation to help people who can only pay you back with thanks, or in trade. With your skill, if making money was your prime concern, you'd be set up somewhere in Beverly Hills, tending the rich."

"Bedford isn't exactly a pocket of poverty," he pointed out.

"No, but Blair Memorial is a strictly nonprofit hospital. That means they do take on patients who can't pay, and perforce, when you're the doctor called in, so do you. That doesn't exactly smack of a man who's out to enrich his retirement portfolio."

He liked the way her mind worked and the fact that she wasn't afraid to display her intelligence. "You're pretty sharp."

She took the comment in stride. "It's my job to be

able to size up people." London winked at him. "See how much they can be coaxed to part with. By the way, you're not sidetracking me. I still want to know why you became a doctor."

Like her smile, the wink went straight to his gut, teasing him. He redirected his thoughts. "Didn't that detective your father hired to investigate me cover that in his report?"

His expression was friendly enough, but she could tell that Reese resented having someone probe into his life without his permission. She didn't blame him.

"He covered facts, not motives." She leaned her chin on her fisted hand. "I'm interested in what makes you tick."

That made two of them, he thought. "Not being particularly brilliant when it came to laboratory science, and having no knack for inventing things that people might want in their future, I figured being a doctor was the best way for me to make a meaningful contribution to society."

Was he really that altruistic, or was he just saying something he thought she wanted to hear? "And that matters to you?"

"Yes," he said honestly, then looked at her, watching the candlelight bathe her features. "Doesn't it matter to you?"

As a matter of fact, it mattered a great deal to her. That was why she conducted fund-raisers for charities rather than for politicians who gave lip service to causes they cared about. It was also why she carefully researched and monitored the charities she was associated with.

But she already knew about herself. What she

wanted to know about was the man sitting across from her. "Don't try to wiggle out of this. We've already done me, now it's your turn." Her eyes sparkled as she looked at him. "Did you like to play doctor as a boy?"

He grinned at her. "Yes."

And she bet the girls lined up around the block to play with him. "I see."

It wasn't what she thought. "With birds and animals." That was how Jake had come into his life. Jake was a stray, a black Lab that some boys in the neighborhood had tortured. He'd tended to the dog's injured leg and had a friend for life.

She didn't quite get the connection. "Then why didn't you become a vet?"

"Beyond being able to mend the obvious, like a broken limb, dealing with animals can be very frustrating. Animals can't tell you where it hurts." And that, he thought, was enough about him. He looked around, changing the subject. "I think your shadow decided to give you the night off after all. I don't see him anywhere around here."

After eighteen months London knew better. She took another bite of her dinner. It only succeeded in getting better with each taste. Too bad men weren't like that, she mused. "Don't let that fool you."

"What?"

She made a circular motion with her fork to include the general vicinity. "Not seeing him. Just because you can't see him doesn't mean he's not there."

She would have a point if the man they were talking about was slight instead of six-six and as solid as a brick wall. "Seems kind of hard to hide someone that big."

A trace of affection came into her voice. Wallace did his best to make this as painless as possible for her. It was just that her frustration got in the way at times. "That's what makes him good at his job."

If Grant could manage to hide himself, that made him *excellent* at his job. "How long has he been your bodyguard?"

"Eighteen months." Her plate empty, she retired her knife and fork.

She was right, he thought, she really could pack it away. Looking at her, his first guess would have been that she ate nothing but fruits and vegetables and sparingly at that.

"Is this a permanent arrangement?"

London rolled her eyes and groaned. "Oh, God, I hope not. Not that I don't like the man," she qualified quickly, "but I was almost rid of him and the others a few months ago—"

"And then what happened?"

She shrugged indifferently, looking down at her plate and the single parsley sprig that was left behind. "A white rose was delivered to my apartment."

Did that have some kind of significance he was unaware of? "I'm afraid I don't follow you."

She was getting ahead of herself. Pausing, she debated just letting the whole thing slide. And then something prompted her to share this piece of her life with this man. This piece no one else knew about except for her bodyguards and her father.

"It was from a secret admirer. Wallace instantly took it to mean something else."

It wasn't a stretch for him. He thought of Monica, a beautiful dark-haired girl he knew in his freshman year at college. "Stalker?"

The speed with which he came to the correct conclusion startled her. "Why would you think that?"

"Was it?" he pressed.

Despite everything, she'd still rather not think that way. "That's what Wallace and my father think, but why would you?"

Then he was right, Reese thought. He felt instantly protective of her. The way he should have been of Monica. She'd been his study partner in bio lab and had poured out her heart to him one evening. She was afraid her ex-boyfriend was stalking her, refusing to accept their breakup. He'd counseled her to go to the campus police. It was the last conversation they ever had.

"I knew someone in college who was stalked."

There was something in his tone that chilled her. She blocked it, the way she did every thought she didn't like, every emotion that came too close.

"And?"

But he shook his head. Monica had a right to rest in peace. "You don't want to know." But *he* wanted to know something. "Was there a note?"

"Yes." More than one. There was even a poem. A bad one, but she found it almost touching in its attempt. "I think it's all pretty innocent, really. If we weren't all so paranoid these days, it would have been just a sweet note, nothing else."

He'd done some reading on the subject since then, educating himself. With stalkers, there were never just one event. "Were there more notes, more flowers?"

She debated saying no, then shrugged. Reese was sharp enough to see through a lie. "Yes."

He appreciated freedom as much as the next person, maybe more, but he found himself shifting sides. Because he'd been the one to find Monica's body behind the library. "Then maybe your father and Wallace have the right idea. It's better to be safe than sorry. Did you tell the police?"

Her father and Wallace had very little faith in the powers of the local police. "Tell them what? That someone sends me white roses occasionally? That his notes are always respectful, almost sweet in nature?"

The waiter appeared just then, a small, black leather folder in his hands that held the bill for their dinner. "Will there be anything else?"

Reese looked at her questioningly. London had already turned down the idea of dessert. She shook her head. "I'm fine."

Reese turned back to the waiter. "That'll be all." The waiter placed the leather folder on the table. Reese took out his credit card and tucked it into the folder. Picking it up, the waiter slipped off to the cash register artfully hidden behind the hostess's desk.

Reese focused on what London had said before the waiter had interrupted them. "He doesn't threaten you, say he wants you for himself, that you belong to him and no one else?" He repeated the gist of the notes that Monica had received.

London shook her head. "No, nothing like that. Personally, I think it's someone who's very shy, that's all, and this whole thing is being blown out of proportion. I deal with a great many people in my profession, Reese. Who knows? Maybe my 'secret admirer' is one of the caterers I work with, or someone in the shop I use to send out engraved invitations. I just don't see the harm—''

He cut her off, a note of passion entering his voice. ''The harm is that this can get out of hand. The harm is that one night this guy might decide that the flowers and the notes have gone on long enough and that it's time for you to make a commitment to him—''

He'd managed to press one of her buttons. She raised her voice to match his. ''Well then, he's out of luck because I'm not in the commitment business, and if he knows anything at all about me beyond my address, he's probably figured that out.''

London's answer wasn't what he would have expected. ''Why?''

She thought he was asking how the person who sent her roses could figure out that she wasn't into commitments. ''Because I'm not with anyone.''

He waved that away. ''No, I mean why aren't you in the commitment business?''

He brought her up short with his question. She raised a brow. ''Getting personal, are we?''

''You raised the point,'' he reminded her. ''I'm just following it.''

She had already made up her mind about him and the part he was going to play in her life. They might as well get this out of the way so he'd know the ground rules. ''I'm not in the commitment business because commitments don't last. Promises don't last. Nothing is permanent.'' She raised her glass. There was just the slightest bit of wine left in it. ''Here's to enjoying the moment while it's here and letting the future take care of itself.''

There was still a drop left in his own glass. He raised it. "To the moment," he echoed.

Reese touched his glass to hers and watched her eyes as she sipped the last bit of wine. Had she been in love and been bitterly disappointed? He couldn't imagine someone walking out on her, breaking her heart, but then, he couldn't envision his father walking out on his mother, either. But it had happened.

The waiter returned, murmured a thank-you and went off. Reese wrote in a tip and signed the slip. Tearing off the bottom sheet, he pocketed it and his credit card.

Setting down her empty glass, London raised her eyes to his and asked, "Well, we've toasted this moment. What would you like to do with the next one?"

He knew what she was asking and she knew his answer before it was given.

Taking her hand in his, they left the table.

Chapter 11

Wallace found a parking space directly across the
street from the apartment building where London
lived and eased his vintage beige Nissan sedan into
it. The remainder of his dinner from Malone's almost
slid off the seat beside him. He managed to catch the
container at the last moment before it fell.

He swallowed an oath as he shut off the ignition
and settled in.

London and the man she was with had left without
warning, their body language giving nothing away
about their imminent departure until they'd stood up.
He'd only had time to hastily throw the contents of
his plate into a container he'd brought with him—the
job had taught him to be prepared. He'd spent too
many hungry nights on surveillance.

Rising to his feet as London and the doctor left the

restaurant, Wallace didn't have time to wait for a waiter to bring the bill. Instead Wallace had tossed money that he knew would more than cover the meal and a small tip down on the table. He would have liked to have had a drink to go with the rest of his meal, but there was no time for that.

Didn't matter, he told himself. His comfort took a back seat to his job.

He glanced at his watch and suppressed a sigh as he leaned back in his seat. It looked as if it was going to be a long night.

But that—he tried to be philosophical—was what the ambassador paid him for.

London stepped into the empty elevator car. Reese joined her, and the door slowly eased closed, locking them away from the rest of the world.

Looking up, she watched the floor numbers change. As they approached her floor, an excitement tingled through her body, leaving nothing untouched.

Her eyes met his.

The excitement increased.

Without any vanity, London thought of herself as sophisticated, a woman of the world. Due to the nature of her life, she had been one for a long time. Women of the world didn't feel their nerve endings jumping in anticipation because of what they hoped might happen between them and a man who might not be part of their world tomorrow.

And yet she did.

And gloried in it.

London couldn't remember the last time she had felt this alive.

Reese walked with her to her apartment. Instinctively she glanced down at the floor before the door, unconsciously bracing herself.

There was nothing there.

The sense of relief was immediate.

"Looking for something?"

London felt a little foolish, reminding herself of her own theory. That the man who left the roses and notes was harmless. She'd allowed Wallace and her father to spook her.

"Just checking. My 'admirer' leaves flowers on my doorstep. Or rather, the doorman does. He brings them up whenever a delivery is made." The descriptions of the delivery boys varied and according to Wallace, they were all legitimate when he checked them out.

"Have you had him checked out? The doorman," Reese clarified when she looked at him. There'd been that moonstruck look on the man's face when he'd complimented her earlier this evening. Maybe the doorman had gotten this job at the apartment just to be close to her. It wasn't out of the realm of possibilities.

She smiled, taking out her key. Her bodyguard was way ahead of him. "Wallace already did that. He's very thorough, very good at his job." Her smile deepened. "The man leaves no suspect unturned." Inserting her key into the lock, she turned it, then looked over her shoulder at Reese. "Did you want to come inside?"

The question was a formality. They both knew he did. And would.

Still, he glanced behind him toward the elevator. It had gone down to the first floor again and remained there. No one was coming up.

"Isn't this about where Grant comes bursting in, whisking you behind the door and slamming it in my face?"

"His job is to protect me from kidnappers and stalkers, not people I choose to be with. I still have some say in my own life," she assured him. "And he knows better than that." She walked inside the apartment, flipping on the light switch. Reese followed her in. "I made it very clear to him that he's to perform his 'duties' tonight at a great distance. Besides—" turning around, she watched Reese close the door "—I told him that I would be safe with you around."

He wasn't altogether sure about that.

Reese picked up a strand of her hair. The softness unsettled him. Aroused him. "And what's to keep you safe from me?"

She raised her eyes to his, the invitation clear. "Who says I want to be safe from you."

He didn't need to hear any more than that.

Very slowly he took her purse from her hand and tossed it onto the table by the door with only his peripheral vision to guide him. He realized only a beat later that he'd come close to knocking over a vase that was there.

His eyes were on her face.

He could feel adrenaline pumping through his veins, could feel his heart rate increasing.

Taking her face into his hands, Reese lowered his mouth to hers and kissed her. Very, very slowly.

It was like having some kind of hallucinogenic drug injected into her blood stream. The reaction was immediate. And intense.

She could feel the effect spreading through her, taking possession of all of her. Hunger sprang into her loins, her limbs, aching for release, for fulfillment. For him.

Her arms went around his neck and she clung to him.

There was no doubt, no hesitation, no place for either. This was right. In this place, in this time, it was right.

The refrain echoed in her brain over and over again.

The kiss grew, the fire rose, fanned by both of them until it was larger than either.

Somewhere in the middle of the swirling abyss the kiss created, London felt her feet leave the ground, felt Reese's arms tighten around her as he picked her up and turned away from the foyer.

She drew her head back to look at him, confusion in her eyes.

"Where's your bedroom?" he whispered, his

throat so tight the words literally had to be pushed through.

It took her a moment to remember. Everything in her head felt jumbled. London pointed toward the rear of the apartment.

He kissed her again, sealing his mouth to hers, and then began walking.

Each kiss he pressed to her lips melted her a little further. Doing the same to him. Sapping his strength a little more.

Reese had the vague sensation of walking for a time. Finally looking up, he saw that they still hadn't reached the bedroom door. It was at the end of the hall.

Curling her body against him, absorbing the warmth of his chest through the clothing—his and hers—that was still a barrier, London looked up at him and saw the smile on his lips. Could taste it even though there was space between them.

"What?"

There was amusement in his eyes. "Your apartment's bigger than the house where I grew up." Not to mention far more elegant. He had a feeling that each piece in it could equal the price of all the furniture his mother had once owned. Certainly the baby grand could.

She wanted to know about that, about the house where he'd grown up.

About him.

About the boy he'd been and even about the

woman who had raised him. Questions filled her head, all manner of questions that surprised her.

Personal questions.

She didn't want this to get personal, wanted only to draw the fun, the pleasure out of it—like eating the sweetest part of an orange—and then toss the rest of it away. It was neater that way. Less complicated. Less involving.

She didn't want to get involved, not at any cost, because it would be too great. She knew that, accepted that.

The questions remained, multiplying. Teasing her. Troubling her.

She blocked them out with a resolve that had been years in the making and sealed her mouth to his with a passion that was calculated to take his breath away. It succeeded in stealing hers, as well.

Kissing her over and over again, Reese lowered her until her feet touched the floor.

Her arms tightened around his neck as she pressed her body to his. The hard contours heightened her excitement. She could feel his desire, feel him want her.

An urgency seized her.

Feeling almost frenzied, she curved her fingers along the lapels of his jacket and pulled it from his shoulders, down his arms. She threw it to the side.

Her fingers flew to the buttons on his shirt.

Catching her hands, he stopped her.

Dazed, London looked up at him in mute confusion. And became lost in the smile on his lips.

''Some of the moves have to be mine,'' he told her quietly.

She swallowed, afraid to draw in a breath, afraid of the moment ending.

Reaching behind her, Reese took the tongue of her zipper and lightly pulled it down the length of her spine. She could feel pins and needles traveling up and down her flesh, breaking every single California freeway speed limit.

Her eyes never leaving his, she shrugged her shoulders. Her dress fell to the floor, pooling around her feet. Displaying her body.

His heart stopped for a split second, then began to beat wildly. She was wearing only thong underwear and black tinted stockings, the kind that came up to her thigh, ending in a flurry of black lace.

He felt his gut tightening so hard, it threatened to snap him in two.

His gaze washed over her, heated, possessive. A sound that could only be termed as appreciative escaped his lips. Cupping her breasts, he drew her close and kissed her throat.

Her head fell back as pleasure filled her and expanded, leaving no space untouched, unlit. She felt as if she could have guided a thousand ships home on her inner light alone.

Her loins ached and she pressed herself against his hardness, eager for the final moment. Wanting gratification the way she had never wanted it before.

It was a long time in coming.

Lowering her to the bed, Reese made love to every

part of her, to her eyes, her cheeks, her hair. To the slope of her shoulders, the hollow of her throat. The curves and dips along her body, caressing, then kissing them. Causing wondrous things to happen along the terrain of her body, wondrous explosions to rack her when she was least prepared.

It was like a wonderful dream.

She never wanted to wake up.

Moaning, trying to maintain at least a shred of decorum, she arched against him as he coaxed each stocking away from her legs. Teasing it from each leg, he kissed each inch that was exposed.

It took a long time for the stockings to finally join her dress on the floor.

Just as she tried to catch her breath, Reese pressed his lips against the small swatch of nylon that still covered her.

She felt the heat of his breath searing into her inner core, making her moist.

Making her crazy.

She couldn't keep from wiggling against his mouth, couldn't keep from arching into him, silently urging him to go further.

To take her further.

When the material seemed to melt away and his tongue found her, she grabbed hold of his shoulders and cried out. The climax was sudden, hard and shook her to the bottom of her soul.

She was vaguely aware of the smile on his mouth as it curved against her skin. Intensely aware of her own need for more.

He brought her to a second climax that racked her body and drained her energy. It took effort for her to even draw a breath.

And then he was above her, his firm body ready for her. Nude, poised.

She realized that she must have somehow clawed away his clothing, but when and how were details she couldn't remember.

All she knew was that she needed him to be with her, to be in her. To take her to the place he'd silently been promising her with every movement of his body.

And still he waited, prolonging the moment. Heightening the anticipation for both of them.

Reese had no idea where all these feelings that were assaulting him were coming from. He was aware of being surrounded, of having every movement choreographed by some unseen power that seemed to be outside his own consciousness.

He was moving to an inner music, an inner fire he had never encountered before.

He wanted to possess her, to feel that final explosive satisfaction that came from having a woman.

He wanted it to continue eternally.

Each time he thought he'd reached a pinnacle, that what he was feeling inside couldn't get any higher, it did. He was not in control here. It was this feeling that had taken over. It was in control of both of them and he could only hang on for as long as possible, enjoying the ride.

Enjoying her.

London felt as if she'd been taken by a huge wave

and carried away beyond the point where she could form coherent thoughts. This was a place where thought and fears could not reach. It was a place that was warm and safe and exciting.

"If you don't take me now," she warned him, her breath coming in disjointed snatches, "I'm going to self-destruct and incinerate right here."

He smiled into her eyes, feeling things he'd never felt before, telling himself it was the moment, not the woman.

"Can't have that," he said, his voice hoarse from wanting her, from the restraint he had been exercising since the moment they'd walked into the apartment.

Because as soon as the door had closed, as soon as he'd looked into her eyes, held her in his arms, he could have taken her there, on her marble foyer, making wild, mindless love to her like the streetwise kid he'd once been.

But she deserved so much more, and if there was only to be this one time for them, he was determined that it was going to be memorable. This much he'd silently sworn to himself and to her.

But the time for promises, silent and otherwise, was over. There was only so much restraint a body could stand, and his was almost past the brink.

It was time.

Balancing his body above hers, Reese used his knee to part her legs, his eyes never leaving her face.

She pressed her lips together, a passenger in the front seat of a roller coaster about to fling itself down a steep incline.

As Reese sheathed himself in her, the power of his entry all but caused him to spin out of control. He brought his mouth down to hers. And for a moment all he did was kiss her, over and over again.

She couldn't take it any longer, couldn't bear to wait, even though she knew she should. London began to move beneath him.

Urged on by her movement, Reese began to move, slowly at first, setting the pace. He could hear her breathing, feel her chest moving as her shallow breaths became shorter. Hear himself as their sounds matched and converged.

Tightening his arms around her, Reese stepped up the pace. A thousand dancing lights surrounded them as they both climbed to the highest crest.

The explosion claimed them both. He heard her cry out his name, felt it echo along his body.

He held her for a very long time, even as the lights in his head faded into the background.

Even as the sound of his breathing slowly leveled itself out.

He wanted to continue holding her until forever descended on them both.

Reese felt he had a good head start.

He knew which windows were hers, had memorized that section on the face of the apartment building. His eyes were instinctively drawn to it whenever he looked up, whenever he kept vigil.

Several minutes after she had entered the building with that worthless cur she'd allowed to accompany her, he watched the lights go out and felt his soul being extinguished.

He knew what was happening, could see it almost as clearly as if it were happening right in front of him instead of twenty stories above.

A guttural sound clawed at his throat, trapped there by sheer force of will.

She'd betrayed him.

He had forgiven her her previous trespasses because their paths had not crossed then, and she could not be held accountable for what she'd done before she'd met him.

But now, now was different.

Now she knew him. Knew he existed.

He'd wooed her, taken the soft, gentle path to her heart. And she did this to him? Gave herself to another man? Let another man touch her, be with her, when by all rights, it should have been him?

It should have been him.

How could she?

Tears stung his eyes as the red flames of rage consumed his sorrow.

He could not tear his eyes away from the darkened windows of her apartment.

The darkness enshrouded him. He felt himself suffocating.

His rage mounted.

Chapter 12

London stirred, realizing that she was beginning to doze off.

The thought that she was comfortable enough with this man to do that ushered in warring emotions. Contentment clashed with fear. As much as part of her was drawn to and yearned for contentment, London knew she couldn't allow herself to let her guard down, couldn't allow herself to reach for feelings that others took for granted. Because she had learned the hard way that those same feelings could leave wounds in their wake that might never heal, that could destroy you.

Awake now, she pulled away from Reese, tucking the sheet around herself. She banked down the ache that was beginning to form within her. "I just want you to know that there are no strings attached."

Her tone was different. The intimacy was gone, re-placed by a distance that belied their proximity. What had changed in the last few minutes, he wondered. He hadn't said anything, hadn't done anything but hold her.

Turning, he looked at her face. There were barriers up. Why?

"I think you covered that in your no-commitment speech earlier this evening."

Edgy, annoyed with herself for going deeper into her soul than she *knew* was safe, London took exception to the word he used. Was he being sarcastic?

"It wasn't a speech," she told him. "I just wanted to make the ground rules clear."

"Ground rules?" His eyes narrowed. Had he mis-read everything that was going on here? "Was this some kind of sporting event?"

She shrugged. The sheet slipped. London quickly tugged it back into place. "Most men would look at it that way."

Had her other lovers? Was that why she'd suddenly pulled back from him? Without allowing himself to get entrenched any further, Reese tried to make sense out of what was being said here.

"I'm not most men, London. I've never found my-self yearning to go along with the mainstream."

She knew that. Sensed that. Despite her struggle to remain behind the lines that had been drawn in the sand, she found herself smiling. London tossed her head, her hair raining over her shoulder. "Maybe that's what I find so attractive."

It was an act, he thought. To what purpose? Self-preservation? Or was she as removed from the scene as her behavior suggested?

"And maybe you should stop playing Rita Hayworth in *Blood and Sand.*"

He was trying to rattle her, she thought. Well, she wasn't going to let him. Wasn't going to allow him to shake her foundation any further than he already had. "Sorry, must have missed that one."

Definitely trying to shut him out, he thought. "I'm surprised, you've got the part down to a T."

There was nothing left for him to do but to get dressed and go home. He had no idea why he didn't, what compelled him to remain. Maybe it was the look in her eyes that he was sure she wasn't aware of. The one that made him think of a vulnerable girl hiding inside a woman's body.

He made her feel fidgety, restless. As if her thoughts just didn't fit into one another. Sitting up on her knees, she drew the sheet up with her. "I just don't want you reading anything into this, that's all."

She made their lovemaking sound casual. Had it been? He hadn't thought so, he had felt a real connection, but maybe he was wrong. "So, do you go to bed with every man you have dinner with?"

Lightning flashed in her eyes. "No."

He'd struck a nerve. Good. "All right, we'll narrow the circle. Every doctor?"

"No." She knew she should terminate the conversation, ignore it, and yet…

And yet some part of her didn't want him to think

of her as the kind of woman she was trying to portray. Some part of her wanted him to know that however briefly it lasted, this had been special.

Was special.

"Then just the ones who save your life." He saw she was about to say something and had a hunch it would be flippant. He gave her the truth. "You went into cardiac arrest on the table."

Her eyes widened. This was the first she'd heard of that. "You didn't tell me that."

"I was saving it." The truth was he hadn't wanted to alarm her and there seemed no reason for her to know all the gruesome details. But maybe she should. Maybe she should come face-to-face with her own mortality. "It helps to have an ace in the hole to play at moments like this."

That sounded far too calculating. From what she'd learned about him, Reese wasn't like that. "You didn't know there'd be moments like this. You're lying."

He wasn't sure if she was referring to her brush with death or to his supposedly saving the information for an opportune time.

"Not about the cardiac arrest. It happens sometimes," he informed her matter-of-factly. "The body goes into shock. There were no aftereffects in your case and I didn't want to upset you." Right from the start he'd had this instinctive desire to protect her. He had no idea why. London certainly didn't seem fragile.

Maybe that was it, he thought. On some level he

could see that she was acting, that the woman behind the facade was fragile.

Silence hung between them. It was time to go. Reese reached for his trousers.

London had no idea why watching such a simple action filled her with such melancholy. Shifting so that she was behind him, she rose up again and pressed a kiss to his neck.

The flow of emotion was immediate, filling his veins, taking possession of him.

Turning, Reese pulled her onto his lap. The sheet she was trying to hang on to was left behind. His arms enfolded her.

"Changing the ground rules again?"

Her heart was pounding. All she could do was look at him. Waiting. Anticipating.

"Playing it by ear as I go along," she breathed.

He knew this wasn't going anywhere, knew it couldn't go anywhere. Neither one of them really wanted it to.

And yet he couldn't help himself, couldn't resist her. So he pretended to play the same game she was playing, with the same nebulous rules. And one rule was that neither of them could be there in the morning.

But for now they had the night, and for now that was enough.

They made the most of it.

One night wove itself into the promise of a next, and a next.

London wasn't sure just how it happened, only that

it did. One moment, Reese Bendenetti wasn't part of her life, and then he was. She still told herself that she could walk away whenever she wanted, just as she had always done before. And since she could walk away, she didn't. She postponed it, confident that when she was tired of the game, the man, the moment, she could just shut down and move on, the way she had whenever a relationship threatened to move beyond the realm of casual fun into something more serious. Until then, she would enjoy herself. Enjoy him.

And as one day slipped into another, she found herself waiting for his call, figuratively holding her breath until she heard Reese's voice over the telephone, caressing her ear. Stirring her.

She found she loved the sound of his voice. Deep, velvety, strong. Everything about Reese Bendenetti fairly shouted "protector." A woman could feel safe with him. Safe, but walking on the edge at the same time. Because the moment his lips met hers, the second his arms closed around her, the illusion of safety disappeared.

The man tasted of danger, of things dark and mysterious. And she loved it.

As long as she knew she could get away when the time came.

Later.

Rachel Bendenetti smiled at the young woman sitting on her living room sofa, the young woman who seemed to brighten the very air that surrounded her.

When Reese had called to say he was coming over and bringing London with him, Rachel had braced herself. Having spent a good deal of her life on the wrong side of the tracks, she knew how the very rich reacted to people who had worked all their lives just to survive.

Prepared to be charitable, Rachel discovered that there was no need to overlook thoughtless remarks and demeaning glances. There were none. London Merriweather, born with a golden spoon in her mouth, was bright, vivacious and honestly charming. Rachel could easily see what it was that appealed to her son.

She was surprised that he had been the one to suggest bringing the young woman who had slipped into his life and his conversation to dinner on Sunday. It was a first.

With all her heart, Rachel hoped it was a sign of things to come.

"It's really lovely to finally meet you, London."

Reese slanted a warning look toward his mother. "There's no finally, Mother."

He had a point, London thought. After all, they'd only been seeing one another for—what was it now?—a little less than a month. She tried to pretend that she didn't know the exact number of days, but she did. Twenty-seven.

Still, she laughed. "Don't tell me that Reese had said so much about me. I won't believe you."

She smiled with her eyes, Rachel thought. That was a good sign.

"He has mentioned you," Rachel allowed. "And it's what he didn't say, more than what he said that caught my attention."

That, London thought, left a great deal of room for speculation. In and of itself it shouldn't have picked up the tempo of her heartbeat. But it did.

She caught the look that passed between mother and son. She could almost visualize what life had been like for them. A struggle, with very little money, but with so much love, it didn't matter. Very little mattered when you had love, London thought.

She'd had opulence in her life, never wanted for anything material, but she found herself envying them. There was an easy communication between them, a communication without words. The kind that she had once enjoyed with her own mother.

London suddenly missed her mother a great deal.

"I can see where Reese gets his mysterious way of phrasing things."

"We just pay attention to things more than some people. And we have our own shorthand." Aware of how that might be taken, Rachel didn't want the young woman feeling shut out and quickly added, "I suppose it comes from having to depend on each other for so long."

Sitting on London's left side, Reese realized that he felt a little tense about this meeting. He wasn't really sure why he had brought London here today. He supposed that part of him felt she needed to meet someone like his mother. That was probably presumptuous of him, but he was a doctor and honor bound to prescribe what he felt his patient needed. London wasn't his patient anymore, but she needed someone in her life like his mother, if only for a few hours. His mother had an uncanny gift for making people around her feel good.

Setting down the tray of refreshments she'd prepared on the coffee table, Rachel went to draw the curtain against the intense afternoon sun. As she took hold of the cord, she looked out and saw a beige car parked across the street from her house. There was a man sitting behind the wheel.

Reese had mentioned that London was being stalked. That was part of the reason for this visit. To put London in touch with a more tranquil way of life.

Rachel turned from the window. "Are you aware that there's a man in a beige sedan across the street?" she asked Reese. "He's watching the house."

London nodded. She picked up the wine cooler Reese's mother had poured for her. "That's my bodyguard, Wallace."

Rachel relaxed, then took a longer look at the man in the vehicle. A man shouldn't have to sit out there all afternoon, roasting in a car.

"Ask him in," Rachel urged. "There's more than enough room at the table and I made plenty."

Wallace did not care to socialize. He'd told London it took the edge off what he did. "Thank you, but no," London declined on Wallace's behalf. "He feels he has a better vantage point if he stays outside,

watching the house. Besides,'' she looked toward
Reese—it was impossible not to feel safe when he
was around, ''I don't think anything'll happen to me
here.''

Rachel smiled and mouthed ''lovely'' to her son
over London's head. Seeing her reflection in the mir-
ror on the opposite wall, London smiled to herself.

Dinner was almost ready. Rachel paused a moment
and perched on the arm of the sofa, looking at her
guest. ''Reese tells me that you hold fund-raisers for
charities.''

Instantly alerted by her innocent tone, Reese knew
where this was going. ''Mother.''

Both women heard the warning note in Reese's
voice. Rachel waved a dismissive hand in his direction as London raised an inquiring eyebrow, waiting
to have the mystery cleared up.

Rachel did the honors. She leaned forward and confided to the other woman, ''He's afraid I'm going to
ask you to do a fund-raiser for Hayley's House.''

''Hayley's House?'' London echoed. She looked
from mother to son and then back again. ''I'm afraid
I'm not familiar with that one—''

''There's really no reason why you should be,''
Rachel said. But she was hoping to change that. The
more people aware of the small facility, the better the
chance that it would receive donations and funding to
keep it going. ''It's just a small place,'' Rachel confided. ''An orphanage, although they have euphe-
misms for that sort of thing now. Bluntly, it's a shelter
for abandoned babies and deserted children found in

hotel rooms, bus stations, alleys, etcetera, thrown away by parents too addicted to some substance or other to realize what they've done—''

Reese watched London's face, attempting to read her reaction. He hadn't brought her here to hear a pitch. He knew how much of her waking hours his mother donated to the facility, but this wasn't the time to draw London in.

''As you can see, my mother's very passionate on the subject,'' Reese told her. ''Once you get her going, there's no stopping her.''

London wondered if he was embarrassed, then decided that he cared too much about the older woman to be embarrassed by her. She rather liked that. He wasn't afraid of what someone else might think.

''That's all right,'' she told him, ''people should be passionate on the subject of charities and helping children.''

Rachel prided herself on being able to spot a lie a mile away. There were no lies here. She grinned as she looked at her son.

''I like this girl, Reese.''

His mother, he knew, liked everyone. But he had to admit it was nice to hear the approval in her voice, even though he was no longer a child but a grown man who didn't need his mother's approval of the woman he chose to spend time with. Still, it was nice to have. God knew he'd gone through his rebellious period. There was a time when he'd given his mother more than her share of grief, although she never complained. She always said that she'd had faith he would come around, even when he hadn't felt that way himself.

"Maybe you'd like to come with me to Hayley's House sometime and look around the place," Rachel coaxed, firmly believing that if you were going for an inch, you might as well try for a mile, or at least a few more inches. "Once you've had a chance to see it, I promise you you'll carry the image around with you for the rest of your life."

All right, she was laying it on a little thick. Reese didn't want London thinking that he'd brought her here with an ulterior motive. "Mother," he warned again.

This time it was London who waved for him to be silent. "I'd like that."

The funny thing was, Reese had to admit she sounded sincere.

And maybe she was, at that.

Rachel beamed at her, ready to accept London into the fold there and then. "Tell me, how do you feel about pot roast?"

London thought of Malone's, the first restaurant Reese had taken her to. A meat-and-potatoes kind of place. Like son, like mother. She grinned. "I don't get it nearly enough."

"Well then, you're in luck." Nodding her head in approval, Rachel rose from the arm of the sofa and went to put dinner on the table.

Conversation for the next few hours was interrupted only long enough to allow one or the other to chew before answering. Otherwise, it went on nonstop over the meal. After dinner, when they were relaxing in the living room, Rachel almost drove Reese from the room by bringing out her beloved album.

The flowers imprinted on the cover had long since faded with age and endless hours of paging through the book. The album featured highlights of her son's life frozen forever in time thanks to the camera she always kept primed and ready. Rachel Bendenetti reasoned that you never knew when the next good picture was coming. Bought the week before Reese was born, it had always been kept within easy reach just in case an important moment came up.

Reese confided that his mother thought almost all moments were important. Rachel made no attempt to deny it.

After spending time giving an informative narrative with every photograph, Rachel retrieved the camera that had made them all possible.

She stood just far enough from the couple to frame them from the waist up.

"Now if you'll just smile for me," she coaxed, the viewfinder against her eye. Lowering it, she peered at the two young people on the sofa. "And scoot together." She motioned with her hand to emphasize her point. "This isn't a wide-angle lens, you know."

Reese looked at London, expecting to hear her demur. She had spent most of her life in front of the camera's eye. He could only guess how she felt about having yet another lens pointed at her.

But to his surprise he saw London move in closer

to him. The next moment she leaned her head against his shoulder.

"How's this?" she asked, smiling brightly.

"Perfect." Rachel snapped two photographs in rapid succession. "The second one's for insurance." She never left anything to chance.

And then it was time to go. London found herself feeling reluctant to leave this safe haven, this small, cozy place where there seemed to be only warmth and joy.

"Now, don't be a stranger," Rachel told her, accompanying them to the front door. Looking at London, she nodded toward her son. "You don't have to wait for Reese to bring you. Just give me a call to make sure I'm home and come on over." She winked. "We can have a little girl talk next time."

The wink reminded her so much of Reese, it momentarily took London's breath away.

"Deal," she promised, a beat before she found herself swallowed up in the other woman's embrace. Rachel was used to being greeted and sent off with hugs that were a matter of custom rather than feeling. Rachel's embrace was so genuine, London was touched.

"You know," she said to Reese as they walked away from the quaint one-story Tudor home, her arm threaded through his, "that's probably the first time anyone's mother sat me down to look at their son's life in pictures."

He'd tried to ascertain whether she was bored or not. He had to admit she had looked as though she was interested. "Sorry about that."

The apology took her by surprise. "No, don't be. I liked it. Liked feeling normal…" She hunted for the right word. "Average."

He laughed as he opened his car door for her. "There's nothing in the world that would make you average, London."

She looked up at him before sliding into her seat. "Why Dr. Bendenetti, are you flirting with me?"

He laughed. "Trying my damnedest."

She waited until he had rounded the hood and gotten in behind the driver's seat. The last thing on her mind was the bodyguard sitting across the street. "Why don't we take this back to my place and see how far you're willing to flirt?"

He looked at her for a long moment. Each time he made love with her, he found himself hungering for the next time, wondering when that feeling was going to end. So far it only grew more intense.

"Be careful what you wish for."

All she was wishing for, she insisted silently, was a passionate evening with a very exciting man. Beyond that she refused to think. There were still no strings, nor would there be any.

Because if there were no strings, there was no risk that they would be broken.

London leaned toward him. "For tonight," she said, her mouth inches from his, "let's not be careful."

Reese had no quarrel with that.

Chapter 13

Control had always been an important part of Reese's life. Control over his body, his thoughts and especially his emotions.

Control had been what had seen him through the days when he'd felt like an outcast because his father had left his mother, because they did without and everyone knew.

But being with London had changed all that. It was as if he'd been freed, unshackled, allowed to finally be himself. An utterly different self he'd never even known existed.

The edginess that had slipped into his vehicle along with them accompanied them all the way to London's apartment building, continuing to grow as each moment went by.

By the time he'd parked the car and they got into

the elevator, he felt the last of his shaky restraint about to snap like a brittle twig.

Reese was vaguely aware that London's bodyguard had made the journey with them in the vehicle that followed in their wake. The man would undoubtedly sense that something was happening the moment he saw them emerge from the car. Reese was sure the tension and electricity that crackled between them was evident to the world at large, but right now, he didn't care what Wallace Grant, or anyone else for that matter, thought.

All he cared about was being with her. In every sense of the word.

She felt it, too, he thought. He could see it in her eyes, in her body language. With each floor that went by, the anticipation heightened.

The moment Reese closed the door to her apartment, shutting out the rest of the world, the explosion rocked them both. Her lips found his. Fingers flew, undoing buttons, unbuckling belts, tugging out shirttails and pulling down zippers.

Doing away with cloth barriers that kept them from one another.

What Reese was most aware of was the intoxicating need he had.

The need that had him.

Not for sex, not for a woman, but for her. For London.

He needed all of her. Her mouth, her eyes, her hair, her thoughts. Every single shred that went into that special magic that was London Merriweather.

Reese was like a man completely consumed with unquenchable desire.

There was always a time, a moment, when in the midst of the tempest that surrounded her, London could suddenly step back, look on like a spectator and revel in being desired, in being needed. She would feel confident in her ability to enjoy and then retreat with no regrets, no scars.

But someone had burned the back stairs and there was no retreat for her, no way out, no out-of-body experience that separated her from the man she was with. She was right there, in the thick of everything, unable to separate her thoughts from her feelings, unable to retreat.

This was all so foreign to her that she felt like a woman possessed.

She felt an overwhelming desire not to be adored, but to give back the pleasure she was receiving, to have and to share. To be completely unlike anything she had ever been before. To feel something unlike anything she had ever felt before.

Each time he brought her up to a higher plateau of sensation, all she wanted to do, even as she reveled in it, was to somehow make sure that Reese would feel that same sensation. That he would be trapped in this fiery inferno of whirling sensations and emotions just as she was.

So she touched, caressed, stimulated, provoked, matching movement for movement. And all the while sinking deeper into the world she was trying to trap him in. Not to exercise her power over him, but so that she would not take this new journey alone.

He took her right there, in the very place he had initially been afraid he couldn't get past the first time they had made love together. Her foyer. Now he was just glad he'd been able to close the door in time. With the cool marble floor beneath her and a chandelier glistening above her, he made London his again, just as she branded him.

It could have been a dirt field for all he cared. All that was important was that she was the one he took with him on the journey to ecstasy.

Eyes intent on her face, trying to memorize every nuance, every expression, he entered her. And was taken by her. It was a partnership, with each silently depending on the other. And glad of it.

He wanted to tell her then, as peaceful contentment slipped over him, over them. Wanted to tell her the word that was throbbing in his throat, begging for release.

Wanted to tell her that he loved her.

But the word remained where it was. Silent. Inside of him.

Loved.

Whether he kept quiet because of instinct, or fear, he didn't know. But the word remained unsaid as he gathered London against him. And prayed for many other nights like this.

''Floor's cold,'' London murmured, her words rippling along his naked chest as she curled her body even closer to his.

He laughed softly, toying with a lock of her hair, marveling at how very soft it felt. How very soft she felt. "I'm surprised it hasn't melted into a puddle beneath us."

She shifted. He felt her lips curve against his chest in a secret smile a moment before she raised her head to look at him. Something warm and giving stirred within him. "I guess we were pretty hot, weren't we?"

"Pretty hot?" He laughed at the weak terminology. "The temperature in hell resembles a skiing resort in comparison." His arm around her shoulders, he pressed a kiss to her forehead. "Would you like to adjourn to your bedroom?"

A small, panicky voice, buried deep inside her, standing on the shoulders of memories, whispered a frantic "No" in reply. She'd already taken too many steps down this road with him. It was time to retreat, to back away before it was too late.

But she nodded her head, determined not to be frightened, not to be cowed.

The next moment she found herself being scooped up in his arms. She laced her arms around his neck. Delighted in the fact that they were both wearing their ardor and nothing more.

She smiled at him wickedly. "A girl could get used to this."

He spared her a look before beginning to walk down the hallway. "That's the general idea."

The general idea. Was he talking about the future?

Please don't promise me something about the future, don't try to give me what no one can.

Somehow she stilled the panic rising in her stomach.

London placed her finger to his lips and warned, "Shhh."

It took him a moment to realize why she was doing what she did. She was telling him that there were still no strings between them. No links to couple them beyond the moment.

He told himself he understood, but he wasn't sure anymore that he did.

Reese kissed her as he walked into the bedroom, passion flooding through his veins. But as he raised his head, something caught Reese's attention. He looked again.

And stopped dead.

There was a flower on her pillow. A long-stemmed white rose. Tucked beneath it was a card.

She saw the look on his face. "What is it?" Twisting around in his arms, London looked toward her bed.

He saw the color drain out of her face.

Setting her down, he crossed to the bed and picked up the note.

"No."

The single word was a stern command to him. He looked at her in surprise, the note in his hand.

London was determined to have no buffers. She couldn't depend on anyone to be there for her of their own free will. To believe that would make her twice as vulnerable as she was at this moment.

"I'll read it. It's addressed to me." Steeling herself, London extended her hand toward him expectantly.

Against his better judgment, Reese handed the small beige envelope to her.

Holding her breath, London opened it and quickly scanned the message. The print could have come from any one of a million printers.

"He's not worthy. No one'll ever love you the way I can."

It was as if the air in her lungs had turned to ice. London let the note drop to the floor at her feet. She felt violated.

Damn it, how had he gotten in here? He had been here, in her apartment, in her room. By her bed.

How?

Reese quickly picked up the note and read it, then looked up at her. He saw the look in her eyes. Fury mingled with fear within him. This wasn't the simple admirer she insisted it was. This was a stalker. "He knows about us."

She nodded grimly. Her voice devoid of all feeling, she said, "He's got to be watching the apartment, seeing us together..."

A chill went over her heart, climbed along her spine.

Reese didn't understand. "How did he get inside? This is a secure building with a security system inside the apartment.'' How much safer could they make her? And yet this scum had managed to get inside.

She dragged her hand through her hair, struggling to get ahold of herself. She felt like pacing, like running, like screaming. She stood perfectly still, torn in all directions.

''I don't know, I don't know.'' Scrubbing her hands over her face, she looked at the pillow. ''Get that out of my sight,'' she cried, waving a hand at the rose.

He took it and the note, putting both aside on her bureau behind the framed photograph of her mother. ''The police are going to want to see them.''

Giving in to the pent-up emotion, she began to pace. ''I don't want the police, I want Wallace.''

''No offense, but the man isn't exactly keeping you safe, now is he? Not if someone can get into your apartment and leave this.'' He nodded toward the things behind the photograph. ''The police have more manpower and resources available.''

He was right, but she didn't want him to be. London wanted fewer people in her life, not more. If the police were brought in, there would be nothing short of a media circus going on around her. It was the last thing she wanted.

She laughed shortly. ''Just what I want, more manpower and resources thrown at me.''

She wasn't taking this seriously. Trying to make her understand how grave the situation actually could be, Reese grabbed London by her shoulders, holding her in place. "This isn't a game, London. Someone wants you—"

It suddenly occurred to her that they were having this discussion without a stitch of clothes on between them. A wanton smile curled along her lips as she desperately blocked out any thought about the man who had invaded her private terrain.

"You mean other than you?"

He knew what she was trying to do, she was trying to divert him. Maybe even divert herself. But for her sake he wasn't going to let it happen.

"Other than me. With possibly very sick intentions. This is serious, London," he insisted. How did he put her on her guard without frightening her? Or was she already frightened and this was the way she was dealing with it? He still didn't know the details that went into making up the whole of London Merriweather. But he intended to, by and by.

Determined to distract both of them, she laced her arms around his neck. "I never argue with a naked man in my bedroom."

Damn it, it was taking everything within him not to succumb to the fact that she was nude and supple against him and that he wanted her with every fiber of his being, potentially serious situation notwithstanding. "It's not a joke, London."

She raised herself up on her toes, brushed a kiss against his lips, needing him at this moment more than she'd needed him all the other moments combined. There was just no getting away from the fact that he made her feel safe. Protected.

"I wasn't laughing."

It was incredibly hard resisting her, harder than anything he'd ever done in his life, but with his hands on her shoulders, Reese moved her away from him. His eyes held hers, the eyes being the only place he could look without feeling his knees grow weak.

"London, we have to call."

London bit her lip and then nodded, a flippant remark dying before she voiced it. She knew he was right. And wished he weren't.

With a sigh she surrendered to logic and the inevitable. "I'll get dressed."

He allowed himself one last sweeping glance. "It's either that or have the detectives fall to their knees in worshipful reverence when they get here."

She smiled then. A real smile that began in her eyes. He instinctively knew how to make her feel better.

"Reverence, huh?"

"Worshipful." He crossed to the doorway. His own clothes were still out in the foyer. He pointed toward her walk-in closet. It was best if they remained separate for a few minutes or neither one of them was going to get dressed. "Now put something on before I forget to be smart about this."

She inclined her head and opened her closet. He'd scored another point in a tally she was keeping almost despite herself. She kept it because she was unconsciously searching for that flaw, that inevitable flaw that all men had.

So far there was nothing on the negative side.

* * *

Wallace frowned as he used a handkerchief to pick up the card.

He'd followed the doctor stoically when the latter had come down to summon him. He had to admit he was surprised that it was the man rather than London who had come. It was obvious to Wallace that she was allowing this relationship to go further than the ones he'd read about in the last bodyguard's report on her.

He'd said very little during the elevator ride up. His words and theories were all for London's ears, not some flavor-of-the-month who had attached himself to her side for a time.

Wallace shook his head as he stared at the note. "How the hell did he get in here?" he stormed, then flushed as he slanted a look at London. "Sorry." He didn't like to curse even mildly in front of her. Laying the note back on the bureau, he blew out a breath, supplying the answer to his own question. "It was probably when I was tailing you earlier."

Wallace stood over London, looking every bit the part of the gentle giant in some outlandish fairy tale. Except that the look in his eyes was not so gentle.

"If you'd let us put up security cameras in the apartment…" he chided her.

Wallace got no further in his reprimand. Her objections still held, even after this. "No. I won't let you do that. I'd feel like I was in the middle of a peep show."

"Maybe he's right," Reese finally said. He'd held

his peace until now, letting London do the talking. After all, it was her life that was in jeopardy, her bodyguard asking the questions. But there was a fine line between brave and foolhardy, and she was being unduly stubborn. ''Better a live peep show than any alternative.''

He noted that Wallace didn't look particularly happy, despite the fact that what he said was actually supporting the bodyguard. But he wasn't here to make Wallace happy, he was here to do what he could for London.

When she said nothing in response, Reese crossed toward the telephone on her nightstand.

Her eyes widened and she quickly darted in front of him, putting her hand on the phone before he could pick up the receiver. ''What are you doing?''

He didn't even bother looking at Wallace, convinced the bodyguard was probably snarling. ''The police, remember?''

She'd let that discussion die away, hoping he would put it out of his mind once Wallace was up here. Obviously, the man had too long an attention span.

''No,'' she insisted. ''I don't want them called in. I've already got three around-the-clock bodyguards. The police can't do any more for me than that, and if the police do get called in, somehow this is going to wind up in the tabloids. I don't want to be on page two.'' There was a slight hitch in her voice that she damned herself for. She didn't want to get emotional about this, just get her point across. ''That'll just bring more crazies out.'' She put her hand on his in supplication. "Please, Reese, I know what I'm saying. No police. Let Wallace and his team handle this." She glanced at Wallace with a look of confidence. "They can keep me safe."

With reluctance Reese released the telephone receiver. He still wasn't convinced that the police couldn't do more than Wallace could, but she did have a point about the crazies. The last thing she needed was a copycat stalker.

"All right," he agreed, his voice low, steady, "but then, I'm moving in."

That had come out of nowhere and for a second it took her breath away. Collecting herself, London demanded, "What?"

He couldn't decide whether she looked like a deer caught in headlights or a tiger about to charge. In either case, Reese didn't want her to think he was taking advantage of the situation.

"You have a spare bedroom. I'll stay there for a few days when I'm not at the hospital." He wanted her to agree. Most of all, he wanted her to be safe. "Call it insurance."

"You're not a professional," Wallace pointed out, grinding out the words so that there was no doubt in Reese's mind just what the man thought of amateurs.

"Doesn't take a professional to care."

Care.

The word hit London smack in her chest, causing an upheaval. Causing panic. He'd just admitted to caring about her. Caring for her. She looked at Reese, wanting to cling, wanting to run, hating the abundance of both feelings that were flooding her. She was supposed to be stronger than that.

"I'll be fine," she assured both men firmly. "I appreciate you two butting heads on my account, and I'm flattered, I really am, but I won't have whoever this is making me afraid in my own home." She looked from Wallace to Reese, wanting to make this point absolutely clear. "He's never threatened me, he's never done anything but be a gentleman." To Reese she said, "Wallace and the team can take care of me, and you can date me. Nothing has to change."

The trouble was it already had, and she knew it and was afraid of knowing it.

But because playing a part made her feel better, she did so.

As was becoming his habit, Wallace took the note and flower with him, intending to put it with all the others.

Softening, hating to have to pull rank, she looked at her bodyguard. "If it makes you feel better, Wallace, you can stand guard outside the door tonight."

The almost boyish face looked unsmilingly at Reese. "How about him?"

Cocking her head, striving very hard for a nonchalant pose, she shrugged.

"He's free to do whatever he wants. If he wants to leave, he can leave. If he wants to stay," she looked at Reese significantly, "he can stay."

The way she looked at him at times turned his mouth to cotton and his knees to water. It took effort to look as if he were unaffected, but he did his best as he shifted his eyes to Wallace. "I'll let you know."

With a swallowed oath about amateurs, Wallace walked out of the room and then out of the apartment. The front door closed a little more loudly than it might have.

Reese had already fixed his attention back to London. "I don't think he approves of me."

She couldn't truthfully argue with that. But then, she doubted if Wallace truly approved of anyone she'd dated. He'd lumped them all under the heading of "security risk." "Don't let that bother you. He's just being my bodyguard. What matters is whether I approve of you."

That sounded like an invitation if he'd ever heard one. "Do you?"

She smiled, winding her arms around his neck. Pressing her body against his. "What do you think?"

As he tightened his arms around her, he realized that she'd put nothing on under the dress she'd hastily thrown on in his absence. The fact that she was naked beneath it made his pulse race. He was beginning to think that wasn't ever going to change. What was more, he was relieved it wasn't.

"I think that you are a lady who is used to getting her own way about everything."

Her smile widened, pulling him into the heart of it. "Handsome and brilliant. I think this time I struck gold."

He would have liked to think, as he brought his

mouth down to hers, that this time would also be the last time for her.

But he knew better than to try to predict what London would do. She seemed to be content with only the moment, and that meant so should he.

The problem was, the moment was no longer enough for him.

Chapter 14

London shifted on the sofa. The newspaper that was sitting on her lap began to slide off and she grabbed it, nearly sending the telephone receiver tucked between her neck and shoulder tumbling after it. On hold, she'd been debating hanging up and calling again later.

But just as she settled back into place, she heard a deep, familiar voice on the other end say hello. It was about time.

"Hi, Dad, it's London. Your daughter, not the city."

It was an old joke, very worn around the edges, voiced at times in exasperation, at other times in memory of a jest her mother had once made when she was trying to get her husband's attention about a matter concerning their only child.

"London, what's wrong?"

There he was, cutting to the chase as he always did with her. No glimmer of the charming chitchat he was known for. Was that concern or impatience she heard in his voice? Probably the latter.

The connection to Madrid was not the clearest, and there was static crackling across the lines, thanks, no doubt to the storm she'd heard was roaming its way across the Atlantic. It had taken her a solid fifteen minutes of transfers once she'd gotten through to the American Embassy in Madrid before she'd been put through to her father's personal line.

It occurred to her that if this had been an emergency, she could have been dead by now. The kidnappers her father claimed to be so worried about would have grown exasperated, given up and dumped her body in the river.

She glanced down at the lead story on the front page of the *L.A. Times*. The story that had prompted her to make this call. Freedom could finally be in her grasp.

"Nothing's wrong, Dad." Absently she traced the outline of the man being led away in handcuffs just below the bold caption. "Everything could be very right. Did you happen to read the front page of your favorite newspaper on the Internet today?"

Except for the subdued crackle, there was silence on the other end of the line. So much so that for a moment London thought she'd lost the connection. "Dad? Are you still there?"

A quiet sigh preceded the ambassador's reply. "I'm here, London. And yes, I read it."

She'd thought that he'd be a little more animated than this. Maybe they weren't talking about the same thing. "They caught the terrorist who kidnapped Susannah Parker. It wasn't any huge network of terrorists, it was just one guy, off his nut, working independently. He's also the one who sent the notes to the other women," she said in case her father hadn't read that far. It was difficult to contain her excitement. "This means we can finally call off the dogs, right?"

"London..." Her father's voice was as serious as she'd ever heard. It was the voice he employed when there was no budging him. "...Wallace called me the other day."

London tried not to scrap her hope. She knew exactly what her father was referring to, what had both Wallace and Reese concerned. Well, damn it, life wasn't without risks, and she was willing to take them in exchange for freedom.

"No offense, Dad, Wallace is a nice man, and there's no doubt he's good at his job, but you do pay him a lot of money to watch me. Did it ever occur to you that he's basing his argument on the fact that he just might want to hang on to this lucrative job?"

Ambassador Merriweather was tired of going around with his daughter about this. Tired of arguing. He'd just spent the past six hours trying to settle a dispute between a major American corporation in Madrid and the minister of industry. He didn't want to have to waste time chasing around this familiar bush with his daughter.

"And did it ever occur to you that your life could be in real danger? That whoever is sending you those notes and flowers is probably deranged?"

The barely tethered anger in her father's voice had her reaching for a dose of protective sarcasm. "Don't think someone can send me notes and flowers without being deranged, Dad?"

Mason nearly lost his temper, something he very rarely allowed himself to do. "This isn't a time for jokes, London. I won't have something happen to you just because you can't take this seriously."

So near and yet so far. Her frustration got the better of her. Rising, she began to pace. "Yes, I know, nothing must happen to the ambassador's daughter. Think of the way that would reflect on you."

"What are you talking about, 'reflect'?" he shouted at her. "I was thinking of how it would feel."

Now there was a word that she wasn't accustomed to hear coming out of her father's mouth. "Feel, Dad? Do you feel?"

"What kind of a question is that?" he demanded angrily. "Of course I feel."

She sincerely doubted he knew the meaning of the word, much less what it entailed. He was the perfect ambassador, the perfect unruffled diplomat. She'd seen a news clip of him several days after her mother's funeral. He was attending the wedding of some prince from one of those tiny countries that most of the world was unaware of. There'd been a

smile on his face. That had convinced her that her
father was completely without feelings.

"What, Dad?" she wanted to know. "What exactly
is it that you feel?"

He had no idea what had gotten into her. Normally,
he told her what he wanted of her, and she eventually
did what was requested. He had no patience with this
rebellious nature she displayed—this trait that was so
like her mother's.

"London, I can't talk to you when you're this
way."

She was through retreating. It was time they had it
out. And if they didn't speak again after it was over,
well, they hardly spoke now, so what did it matter?

"No, you have to talk to me when I'm this way.
Not talking to me has *made* me this way. Sending me
away from you when Mother died made me this way.
You sent me away when I needed you."

He wasn't accustomed to having to explain himself
to anyone who wasn't part of the government. "I sent
you away to spare you."

That was a lot of hogwash, something he'd told
himself to ease his conscience, London thought.
"Spare me what—contact with the only person who
could have seen me through that awful time?"

She'd been eight years old. What did she know of
going on without someone who was a vital part of his
everyday existence? Someone who had been his guid-
ing sun? Children bounced back, their hearts didn't
break the way adult hearts did. He'd sheltered her and
expected her to be fine.

Each word felt heavy as he dug it out. "I was having a terrible time adjusting to life without your mother. I didn't want you to see me like that."

His admission took London by surprise. He'd actually felt something, felt a loss? Resentment crowded her. Damn it, why hadn't he said so? Why hadn't he told her? It would have meant so much.

"Seeing you like that would have helped me, would have made me feel that we both missed her." She took a deep breath, her voice suddenly shaky with emotions she didn't want to release. If he was telling her the truth, then his so-called restraint had cost them both. "And maybe it would have brought us together the way she'd always wanted us to be."

London was right, he realized. She was right. And there was nothing he could say to change that. "London."

There was another long pause, this time it was hers. "Yes?"

"I'm sorry."

This was her father; she wasn't going to read anything further into his words. "Sorry we're having this conversation, or—"

He broke in. "Sorry that I didn't realize how much you were hurting, too." He took a deep, steadying breath. That out of the way, he still was not going to be moved. "But that's still not going to make me terminate Wallace and his men."

She supposed, if she looked at it from his perspective, she could see his point of view. "No, I don't suppose it will." London could hear someone in the background, calling to her father. She was surprised that there hadn't been an interruption before now. This probably ranked among the longest conversations they'd ever had. "I guess that's the rest of your life calling. You'd better answer it."

He had to go, but since they'd cleared things up this far, he had one more thing to attend to. Something that had gone unsaid for perhaps too long. "One last thing, London. You do know I love you, don't you?"

He'd never said that to her before, although her mother had told her he loved her more than once. She'd just assumed her mother was covering for her father, the way all good mothers did.

London felt a smile creeping up from her toes. "I do now."

The connection was suddenly lost. She figured the storm was having its way with the phone lines. Her smile didn't abate. She hadn't won what she wanted, but she'd gotten something far more precious. The impossible had happened. She and her father had cleared the air.

Mentally she reviewed her calendar for the coming month. Maybe she could manage a trip to Madrid around the third week or so. It was a thought.

On her way to the first-floor tower elevators, Alix DuCane turned the corner and just barely avoided colliding with Reese, who was coming from the opposite direction. Both halted abruptly within inches of contact.

The first thing she noticed was that he was smiling.

To her knowledge, he wasn't given to looking like that for no reason.

"Well, you're looking pretty chipper today," she commented. Rooting around for a cause, she thought of the surgical list she'd seen at the nurses' station just beyond the operating rooms. "I take it that bowel resection you performed this morning went well."

He laughed. The surgery had gone far better than anticipated. "Yes, but this has nothing to do with a bowel resection."

No, she thought, surgery didn't put a light into a man's eyes, even an excellent surgeon's, like Reese. She wasn't about to let him get away without telling her what did.

"Tell me." She placed her hand on his arm to add weight to her entreaty. "I could use a little happy news."

Reese made no reply. Instead he dug into his pocket and took out a ring box. When he opened it, there was a blue-white, heart-shaped diamond nestled against a black velvet interior.

It took her breath away. "Wow." Alix looked up at him. "Reese, I don't know what to say. This is so sudden. We're not even dating." She saw the sudden bewildered look on his face and laughed. "Relax, I'm kidding." And then she became serious, wanting to share in his happiness. "Who's the lucky girl? I didn't think you ever got to see anyone except for your patients." And then, as she mentally backed up, it hit her. "It wouldn't be that gorgeous one who was brought in the other month, the one who'd tried to find a way to drive through a telephone pole, would it?"

Reese had always maintained that Alix had one of the sharpest minds at the hospital. The brightest of the bright. "You do take all the fun out of things, Alix."

Overjoyed that he'd found someone to share his life with, Alix gave him a quick hug.

"But if I know you, you'll find a way to put it right back in."

She stepped back to admire the ring again. The overheard lighting threw blue-white sparks everywhere in the corridor. "So when's the big day so I can clear my calendar?"

He flipped the box closed and slipped it back into his pocket. "Haven't asked her yet."

That was so like a man. "Well then, get to it. Not that I expect any woman in her right mind to turn you down," she added. And then a thought hit her. Her grin grew wider. "Oh, God, Reese, your mother is going to be so jazzed about this. Have you brought the lady around to meet your mom yet?"

He thought of the first encounter. After a few minutes he might as well not even have been there. "Not only has my mother met her, she's assimilated her. You know that orphanage my mother volunteers at?"

"Hayley's House?"

Alix had gone and held and fed a few babies there herself when time permitted. She'd also volunteered her professional services on occasion.

Reese nodded. "That's the one. Mom's taken her there several times already. She even corralled London into holding a fund-raiser for the place next month."

Alix laughed. Rachel Bendenetti had never struck her as being a shrinking violet.

"Sounds like this is a good match all around." She had to get going. Alix brushed a kiss against Reese's cheek. "I am really happy for you. Now put that ring on her finger, Romeo, and get on with it, already."

He intended to do just that this evening.

Reese made reservations at the most expensive restaurant in the area.

He wanted to propose there, where the lighting was romantic and the atmosphere even more so. There was even a band playing tonight. He knew London liked to dance.

The plan was to give her the ring just before the dessert arrived.

That was the plan. But he couldn't wait.

Tension was all but taking the very air out of his lungs. He was pretty sure London would say yes, but there was still a small part of him that was afraid the evening, the proposal wouldn't go the way he hoped it would. Afraid that after all this time, he'd found the girl of the dreams he didn't even know he had, and she would turn him down.

So when London opened the door in response to his knock that evening, he decided the hell with timing and plans. It was better to get this over with and then take her out to celebrate.

If there was something to celebrate.

Whenever she went out with Reese, London was prepared for a phone call telling her that he'd be delayed because of an emergency. Seeing him standing there brought an instant smile to her lips. At least the evening was off to a good start, she thought. And with any luck it would end that way, too. In her bedroom.

"Hi, you're early." London turned toward the hall table where she'd left her things. "I'll just go get my wrap—"

His heart thumping against his chest, Reese caught her arm, stopping her. "Wait a second."

She turned around obligingly. Her smile faded slightly when she saw the serious look on his face.

Oh, God, he was going to break up with her.

Well, it wasn't as if she hadn't been preparing for this from the first moment he'd walked into her life. More than half a lifetime of training was hard to shrug off. Still, something within her felt as if it was about to go into mourning.

"Yes?"

Now that he had her attention, he felt his mouth go dry, and he forgot all the words he'd been rehearsing.

"I'm not sure how to say this."

She was surprised at him. Didn't doctors advocate ripping off a Band-Aid in one fast motion? This was just like that. Swift if not painless.

"Just spit it out," she told him. "That's the best way. It doesn't have to be fancy. It just has to be said." Although she wished it didn't. She wanted a little longer, just a little longer. Happiness had made her greedy.

Reese was disappointed in himself. Granted, he had never exactly been eloquent, but he'd never been tongue-tied, either. This was a side of himself he wasn't happy about.

"I really thought I would be better at this. Not that I've had any practice," he added quickly.

The last thing he wanted was for her to think he'd done this before. He'd never proposed, never wanted anyone in his life on a permanent basis before. Until London had come into his life, he was certain that he would just go through it doing all the good he possibly could and that would be enough.

After having met London, he knew it wasn't enough. Not anymore.

He looked so uncomfortable she suddenly found herself wanting to put him out of his misery. "Do you want me to make it easy for you?"

He looked at her sharply. "No."

Reese had no idea what she could do, other than propose herself. He didn't want her beating him to the punch. He wasn't a traditionalist, but there were some things that a man had to do first.

His fingers curved around the velvet box in his pocket. Now or never. If he kept on babbling this way, she was going to think he was certifiable.

He took a deep breath and plunged in. "London, I'd like you to wear something for me."

Had the breakup made a U-turn? Or was this about something else? The conversation she'd heard earlier today with her bodyguard came back to her. "What, a two-way homing device? Sorry, Wallace already proposed that, and I—"

He had no idea what she was talking about, only that he was about to start perspiring if he didn't get this said soon. "No, this."

Taking her hand, he placed the box in it.

Stunned, London stared for a long moment at the black object nestled in her palm.

He wasn't leaving her. He was staying. Saying he was staying permanently.

She didn't know which was worse.

Because as painful as it would have been to see Reese leave, what he was asking of her made things even more difficult. He was asking her to believe that this was going to continue. That they were going to continue. Asking her to believe, when she knew things didn't continue. They ended. For her they always ended.

He couldn't read her expression. She was just standing there, looking at the box. "Aren't you going to open it?"

She didn't want to open it, didn't want to see it. Didn't want to slide down deeper into the quicksand from which there was no escape.

"No." She pushed the box back into his hand. "Let's just go out to dinner, Reese." Again she turned to retrieve her things on the table. "They're not going to hold the reservation indefinitely, even for the doctor and the ambassador's daughter—"

Confused by her reaction, he took hold of her arm, turning her back around to face him. "Maybe you don't understand—"

That was when the need for self-preservation suddenly leaped in between them. "Yes, yes, I do understand. I understand perfectly. You're giving me a ring, or a skate key, or some kind of binding thing and asking me to be part of your life—"

She sounded as if she were accusing him of something. Why was this going so wrong?

"I'm asking you to marry me so we can be part of each other's lives," he insisted.

"We already are," she told him. Didn't he see that? He was the first thing she thought of every morning, the last thing she thought of every night. And she wasn't happy about it. "Why can't you just leave things the way they are?"

There came a time when commitments were made, when people settled down. They'd reached that junction. He thought, hoped, they'd reached it together. "Because I don't want to take it one day at a time anymore."

She shook her head adamantly. "That's the only way I know how to take it."

"I want forever, London." He didn't know how to say it any better, any plainer than that.

Cornered, trapped, she lashed out, trying to make a break for freedom. "What kind of doctor are you? Didn't they teach you anything in doctoring school? There is no such thing as forever."

All right, she was being incredibly practical, especially for London. "Then I want as long as I can get."

"That's what I'm giving you," she cried. Didn't he see that? Didn't he know what he was asking of her? To strip herself bare and leave herself exposed to a pain that was more than she could endure? "One day at a time. It's all I can give you. All you can give *me*. Anything else would be a lie."

She was shouting now, and he tried to break through the barriers she was throwing up between them. "It doesn't have to be that way."

"But it is." Suddenly she was very, very tired. He was boxing her in and she wanted to escape. "Look, maybe going to the restaurant isn't such a good idea right now." She laced her arms in front of herself protectively. Blocking him out. "I'm suddenly not hungry. I just want to be alone for a while."

There was an edginess in her voice. He was accustomed to her being in complete control of herself, confident, poised. She was none of those now. And her body language was telling him that she was walling herself off from him.

"Will you just go? I need my space."

He tried to take her into his arms, but she backed away. Reese felt frustration welling up inside of him. "I'm not going to crowd you, London."

"Then go. Please." Her hands on his chest, she pushed him to the door. "Please."

There was nothing else he could do. He slipped the ring box back into his pocket. Squaring his shoulders, Reese opened the front door and left.

Chapter 15

He'd never known two days to drag by so slowly. Filled with work, both of the emergency and non-emergency variety, the minutes of each day still moved with the speed of two anesthetized turtles.

Reese put in for an extra shift, not wanting to go home. Nothing worked.

Try as he might to crowd his head with thoughts that had nothing to do with London, all his thoughts had something to do with London.

He'd never placed himself on the line before and so had never suffered rejection before. He couldn't say he cared for it much.

Sitting at the desk at the fifth-floor nurses' station, Reese closed the folder on the patient being released today. His cell phone rang and he welcomed the diversion.

"This is Dr. Bendenetti."

"I still get a thrill hearing you say that."

He recognized his mother's voice and wondered what she was doing calling him here. His mother never called the hospital, never called his cell. He felt an odd premonition.

"Reese, I'm sorry to call you on your cell phone, but do you know where London is? I'm worried about her."

That made two of them, but for entirely different reasons, Reese thought. He had no idea where London was. He hadn't seen her since she'd turned down his proposal. Initially he'd thought of going back, but to what end? To yell at her? To try to coax her into changing her mind? Neither seemed the right way to go. So he remained away, working. It was what he was good at. Relationships obviously weren't.

"No, Mother, I don't know where London is." He told himself to drop it there, that anything concerning London was no longer his affair. For all he knew, she was snubbing his mother. Having turned down the son, she might not want to have anything to do with the mother. It seemed like a fair guess. But something prompted him to ask, "Why?"

"Well, I stopped by on the way to Hayley's House to pick her up the way we'd agreed, but she's not answering the door. It's not like her to stand me up."

How could his mother possibly know what was or wasn't like London? Granted she was pretty good at sizing people up, but she hadn't known the other woman for that long.

How about you? Certainly didn't take you long to propose, did it? an inner voice taunted him. "Are you sure you got the day right?"

"Of course I got the day right," Rachel replied patiently. "I never forget anything, you know that."

Yes, he knew that. His mother had a memory like a steel trap. She always had. "Maybe she just forgot." But even as he said it, he knew it wasn't true.

It was as if his mother could read his thoughts. There'd been a time, when he was young, when he'd been convinced of it. "That isn't like her, either."

No, he thought, his mother was right. That wasn't like London. And it really wasn't like London to take anything out on his mother that might have happened between them. He was just looking for excuses, but in truth, there weren't any.

"Did you see any of her bodyguards around?" Maybe whoever was on duty had just gone shopping with London. Or maybe, the thought suddenly occurred to him, London had been in another accident.

"Not unless they're disguised as potted plants or paintings." Rachel's voice grew serious. "Reese, I'm worried. London didn't seem to be concerned about whoever was sending her those notes, but I am. This is a very strange world…"

So she'd shared that with his mother had she? That meant that London was more concerned about the notes than she let on. That bothered him.

"All right, go home, Mother." He tried not to allow his own mounting concern to enter his voice. "I'll see if I can find her after my shift's over."

"Call me the moment you do." He wasn't fooling her. She knew him too well. He was as worried as she was. Rachel paused before adding, "I've got a bad feeling about this."

The trouble was, Reese thought as he flipped closed his cell phone, his mother's bad feelings were usually right.

This was absurd, Reese told himself as he rode up in London's elevator some thirty minutes later. He was getting worked up over nothing. The woman could look after herself and even if she couldn't, she had a tag team of bodyguards who could. Nothing had happened to her, she'd just forgotten an appointment. Lots of people forget appointments.

Still, he had seen the rose on her pillow that evening, had seen how pale London had grown when she'd discovered it.

What if…?

Determined not to let his thoughts go there, Reese got out of the elevator and went to her apartment. He rang the doorbell, but no one answered. Not that time nor the ten times that followed in quick succession.

There was no one home.

But there should have been. He'd asked the doorman before coming up if the man had seen London today. The answer had been a firm no. When he'd pressed, the doorman had informed him that he had been on duty from ten this morning until now, and in that time he had not seen her in the building, much less walking out of the building.

Still, the man had to take a break sometime. Maybe London had left then.

Damn it, he was letting this all get to him. There could be a hundred explanations.

He kept coming back to one.

Since she obviously wasn't answering her regular phone, he took out his cell phone and called hers.

There was a moment's delayed reaction before he realized that the ring inside his cell phone was being echoed from within the apartment. Her cell phone was in there.

The knot in Reese's stomach tightened a little more. London was never without her phone. She'd told him she felt naked without it. Either she was inside and not answering for some reason, or—

Reese struggled to curb his initial instinct and not run down the fifteen flights of stairs to the ground floor. Instead he forced himself to take the elevator down. Bursting out through metal doors that were barely parted, he quickly hurried over to the doorman.

"I want you to let me into London Merriweather's apartment."

The other man drew himself up to his full five foot eight. He figured the several inches he lacked were made up for by the uniform he wore. "Hey, look, mister—"

Reese didn't have time for an argument. He said the first thing that came to his mind. It was either that, or grab the man by his lapels and slam him against the opposite wall.

"I'm her doctor and I think there might be a medical emergency.'' Reese already had his wallet out and flipped it open to show the doorman his hospital identification. ''There's no answer from inside the apartment, but I heard her cell phone ringing. She is *never* without her cell phone,'' he emphasized as the doorman began to mount a protest.

Faced with the look in Reese's eyes, the doorman had no recourse but to back down.

''Okay, sure.'' He swallowed nervously as he went to the front desk and unlocked the drawer where all the keys were kept. ''But you're taking full responsibility for this.''

Reese was already shifting impatiently on his feet, ready to take off. ''I'll sign in blood if you want, just get up there.''

The apartment was empty.

There was no response when he called her name, nothing but the faint echo of his own voice.

''Looks like she's not here,'' the doorman volunteered timidly. He made no move to leave his post right outside her doorway.

But Reese wasn't so sure. He raised his hand in silent dismissal as he went to look through the rest of the apartment.

London wasn't in any of the other rooms.

Puzzled, worried and annoyed with himself at the same time, Reese made his way back to the front door. As he reentered the living room, something crunched beneath his shoe.

Looking down, he saw that it was a piece of a vase.

He recognized it as the one he'd almost knocked over that first night he'd made love to her in her apartment. Where was the rest of it? Had it fallen? Or was there some kind of a struggle here?

Was Wallace out looking for her? Was that why the bodyguard wasn't here?

"Ready?" the doorman asked nervously. He kept looking over his shoulder, worried that the manager might be coming up, or that someone else on the floor might see him and make a report to the manager. He couldn't afford to be let go. "You know, this could mean my job if—"

But Reese wasn't ready to leave just yet. He really didn't even know why, but he suddenly felt an urgent need to find the rest of the vase.

"Wait."

Leaving the doorman, Reese hurried into the kitchen and looked inside the lower cabinet where London stored her wastebasket. The pieces of the vase were inside, neatly thrown away. He took the wastebasket out. Something red caught his eye, and he lifted out a piece.

There was blood on the long jagged edge.

Hers? Had she cut herself picking up the pieces? Or was something else going on?

Had the vase been thrown at someone coming at her?

His heart froze.

"Hey, Doc, you coming?" the doorman called out to him.

He put the basket away beneath the cabinet and

crossed to the front door again. The doorman quickly locked up and was at the elevator bank in record time, pressing for the down button.

"Are you sure you didn't see London leave?" Reese asked just as the car arrived.

The doorman was the first in. He pressed for the first floor, relieved the ordeal was over. "I already told you, I was at the front entrance all day."

Front entrance. "Is there a back entrance?" Reese asked quickly.

The question clearly threw the other man. "Well, yeah, but that's for the delivery people. Ms. London wouldn't take that." He made it sound tantamount to her slumming.

"Not of her own free will," Reese said, more to himself than to the man with him. He dug into his pocket and gave the doorman a twenty. They'd reached the ground floor and the lobby. "Do you know where her bodyguard lives?"

The doorman thought for a moment. "Don't know about the other two, but if you mean Wallace, yeah, I know where he lives. He's got an apartment over on Grand Avenue in Santa Ana. One of the older buildings. Told me he was saving up to move down to El Toro."

With the kind of money Reese figured the ambassador was paying Grant, the bodyguard could easily have moved to a more upscale area. "What's the address?"

The doorman waited until another twenty appeared to keep the first bill company before he rattled off Wallace's address.

Wallace wasn't at his apartment.

Feeling desperate, Reese knocked again, then tried the doorknob. Something sticky met his touch. When he examined his hand, there was blood on it. Fresh blood.

He thought of the vase.

The sick feeling in his stomach grew. What was going on here?

Like a man possessed, he ran down the narrow staircase to the first floor, the metal stairs echoing each step he took.

Reese used the same story on the superintendent that he had on the doorman in London's building. And the same bribe.

The superintendent, a small, shapeless man with two days' gray-and-white growth unevenly sprouting on his face used his spare key to let Reese into Wallace's apartment. Unlike the doorman he had no compunction about coming inside with him. He liked to look, to snoop, whenever possible. A man needed to know about the people he rented out to. That was what the building owner paid him for.

This time the superintendent got more than his money's worth.

The old man's jaw dropped as he walked over to a mural, drawn like a moth to a flame.

"Wow, he must really have the hots for that woman," the older man marveled, moving closer to take in as much as he could without putting on his glasses. The wall was crammed with photographs and news clippings about London. Curious, he turned to Reese. "She anybody?" he wanted to know, then pressed, "You know her?"

Reese felt as if he'd just been gut shot.

The photographs all collided into one another, a haphazard collage. There were some pictures that had obviously been taken several years ago, but most were recent.

His eyes honed in on a photograph that had to have been taken within the past few weeks. It was the evening he had taken her to Malone's. He could tell by the dress she was wearing.

His head had been cut out.

"Yes," he said quietly to the superintendent, "I know her."

The man cackled, shaking his head. "Wish I did." He looked around, disappointed that the other walls were not similarly decorated. "Wonder if he's got any more pictures or stuff in that storage room he's always so secretive about."

The half-muttered question sent up a red flag. Reese all but grabbed the other man by the shirt. Adrenaline began to pump madly through his veins. "What storage room?"

The man jerked a thumb down, indicating a spot below his feet. "The one in the basement."

"There's a basement?" As far as he knew, the homes and apartment complexes in Southern California didn't have basements.

"This is an old building," the superintendent reminded him. "Different code then. Lucky thing for some of the tenants. They pay extra to have it. I told Grant I needed a key to the place, but he said no, that there was this sensitive equipment there and he didn't want anyone fooling with it." The man snorted indignantly. "Like I'd fool with—"

Reese didn't have time to listen to the other man rave. "Take me to it."

But he remained where he was, shaking his head. "Won't do any good. I told you, I ain't got a key, and he keeps it padlocked. Doesn't trust nobody."

There's a good reason for that, Reese thought. The man was a monster of a magnitude that far transcended any physical flaws. "Do you have bull cutters?"

The superintendent knew where he was heading with this. He led the way back into his apartment and went into his tool chest, a massive red affair with multiple drawers and crannies mounted on wheels.

The bull cutters were inside the cabinet. He took the set out gingerly. "But that's against the law," he protested.

As if the man cared. "We want the law," Reese told him. "Once we're down there, I want you to point out which storage room is Grant's and then go call the police—911," he emphasized.

"Why?" The man's deep-set, mud-colored eyes opened up wide. "What'll I tell them?"

That was a no-brainer. Opening the door to the stairwell, Reese led the way down to the basement.

"Tell them to get down here as fast as they can. Tell them a woman's life is in danger."

The superintendent was right behind him. They stopped as they came to the landing. "What woman?"

He didn't have time to write out a cue card for the man. Every second he was here talking to him might be a second that was crucial in saving London's life. He grabbed the bull cutters the superintendent was still holding.

"Which one is it?" Unnerved, the unshaven man pointed to the third door from the wall. The largest one. Reese took off. "Just get them here," he tossed over his shoulder as he ran. "Fast."

Reese approached the storage room door. His heart was in his throat.

Logically, he should wait for the police. But logic didn't have anything to do with the situation right now.

Why hadn't he seen it?

London was being stalked by her own bodyguard, by the very man who'd been paid to look after her. That was why he'd managed to get into the apartment without setting off any of the alarms. He'd been the one to install the security system in the first place.

All the while he'd been entrusted with keeping her safe, he'd been a breath away from abducting her. How sick was that?

As he brought down the bull cutters on the padlock, Reese prayed that he'd find London here. Alive. If she wasn't here, he hadn't a clue where to start looking for her.

The padlock fell to the floor.

Reese threw open the door. The enclosure looked like a tiny model home, all stuffed into an eight-by-ten area. There was a bed, table and chairs and a sofa arranged before a small television set.

All the comforts of home, Reese thought sarcastically.

A musty smell assaulted his nose. There was a single bulb hanging overhead, illuminating the tiny, pseudo-living space. It was just dim enough for him to need a moment to get his bearings.

Just long enough to hear the desperate, almost inhuman sound.

And then he saw her.

London.

She was bound hand and foot and tied to a chair over in one corner. Her mouth had been sealed shut with duct tape.

She was wearing a wedding dress. A veil drooped over her left eye.

"Oh, my God." His heart pounding, Reese dropped the bull cutters, raced over to London and pulled off the tape.

Pain shot through her, going from her face to the top of her head. It was worth it just to be free of the damned tape. London gulped in air as Reese worked to free her of the ropes.

"It's him. It's Wallace," she cried, fighting back hysteria and the dizzying realization that she'd been rescued. "He's the one who's been sending the poems, the flowers, everything. He said he had to do something before someone like you took me away from him."

Reese untied the rope from around her ankles. Freeing her, he pulled London to her feet. He wanted to hold her, to comfort her, but they had to get away before Grant returned. "Where is he now?"

She almost cried at that. The whole thing had been too horrible to describe coherently.

The words almost refused to emerge. "He went out to get us our wedding supper."

She'd always considered herself strong, but London struggled to keep from shuddering. She'd trusted this man, allowed him into her home, into her life, for the past eighteen months. And all the while he'd been fantasizing about her, planning this. Bit by bit.

How could she ever trust anyone again?

"He said we could marry each other, that all we needed to do was say the words and then he'd be my husband and would always take care of me."

Reese saw the tears in her eyes. For now, he made no mention of them. "When did he leave?"

She shook her head. "I don't know." Time had become a blur. "Ten, fifteen minutes, maybe longer. I didn't have any way of telling."

"That's all right," he assured her, needing her to remain as calm as she could. He didn't want her to fall apart now. "The police are on their way." Reese saw her wobble. "Can you walk?"

Her legs felt numb, the ropes had all but cut off

her circulation. But she needed to get out of here before she suffocated. Determination entered her eyes. "I'll crawl if I have to."

"Then let's get out of here."

Reese took her hand. London winced involuntarily. He looked down and saw that there were red, raw lines around her wrists where the ropes had bitten into her flesh. It wasn't difficult to guess why. London had tried to work the ropes off her wrists.

A rage bubbled up inside him.

The next moment London was yanking on his arm, pulling him back from the entrance.

Her eyes were huge as she stared past his shoulder. There, in the doorway, was Wallace.

Chapter 16

His plans were being thrown all awry.

Bendenetti, always Bendenetti. Why couldn't the bastard just stay away?

The expression on Wallace's face was one of sheer malevolence. "Where the hell do you think you're going?" he demanded, his bulk blocking the only way out.

Reese's hand tightened on London's in silent reassurance. "Get out of the way, Grant. The police will be here any minute."

A look Reese couldn't even begin to describe entered the bodyguard's eyes. The man looked enraged, deranged. Reese moved his body in front of London.

"The hell they are." As his own words echoed back to him, Wallace's eyes shifted toward London.

For one slim second a contrite look passed over his face. "Sorry. I shouldn't curse in front of you."

"You shouldn't stalk her, either," Reese told him angrily.

The hatred returned in flaming sheets of rage. He'd always hated pretty boys. The ones who were better at things than he was. The ones who had all the advantages he never had. Wallace curled his fingers into his palms, trying to contain the rage.

"It wasn't stalking, it was courting," he spat out. "I had to do something. She was going to talk her father into dismantling security, into sending me away." Forgetting Reese, Wallace looked at the only person who mattered in this. London. "Don't you understand? I have to be near you. You're all I think about, London, all I want." His eyes pleaded with her to understand. "I'll be good to you, I swear. You'll never want for anything, never feel afraid again. I'll protect you." The emotion in his voice swelled with each word he uttered. "And I won't ever, ever leave you."

He knew her fears, her thoughts. London felt violated, as if he'd found a way to crawl into her mind.

It was hard to keep the revulsion from her face.

"I know all about the way you feel, about being abandoned. I was, too." Wallace was sure that if he just kept talking, she'd see that they were soul mates. He had to make her understand that they belonged together. "I grew up in an orphanage. Don't you see, we were meant to be together." His eyes, soft only a second before, hardened as they shifted toward Reese. "And no one else is ever going to have you."

Numb, incredulous, London stared at Wallace, saying nothing.

His patience at an end, Wallace suddenly reached past Reese, shoving him aside. He grabbed London's arm. "Let's go."

London literally dug in her heels, but even so, she could offer little physical resistance to the big man's strength. All she had was her own strength of will. He wasn't going to do this, wasn't going to take her again. She couldn't let him. "No!"

Reese grabbed his other arm, trying to pull him away. "Let her go, Grant."

In response, Wallace swung around and hit Reese's jaw, hard. The force sent Reese flying head first against the wall. The blow to his head jarred his teeth and very nearly rendered him unconscious as he crashed to the floor. For a moment his body was too stunned for him to collect himself.

"I haven't got time for this now, London," Wallace told her, scooping her up into his arms. "This is for the best, you'll see. I promise."

Doubling up her fists, London beat on his chest. Though she was no weakling, it was like a fly assaulting a rhino.

"Wallace, put me down!" she ordered. "You can't do this. It's not right."

"You're wrong. Nothing's ever been more right," he said.

His arm tightening around her, he turned toward

the entrance. His car was parked just outside the building, and they could still get away. He could marry her later, but he had to save her for himself now.

Behind him he heard Bendenetti moan. The only fly in the ointment. As long as the other man was alive, he would never completely possess London. Bendenetti had to be eliminated.

Holding London against him like a doll, Wallace pulled out the gun he had tucked into the back of his pants with his free hand. "Cover your ears, London."

London's heart stopped when she saw the weapon. He was going to kill Reese. "Wallace, please," London begged. "Don't do this. I'll do anything you want, just don't kill him."

Anything he wanted. Which meant she loved the other man. "I have to. He'll come after you and he won't stop." Cocking the revolver, he took aim.

"No!" London screamed, grabbing his arm. She jerked it upward, and the shot went wild, going through the ceiling. Wallace cursed loudly. The next second London dug her nails into his eyes, and he screamed in pain.

Still dazed, his own vision double, Reese scrambled to his feet. He nearly tripped over the bull cutters. Picking them up, he held them with both hands and swung the heavy tool with all his might at the back of Wallace's head.

The big man crumpled to his knees, then fell on top of London. She screamed.

His head still spinning from his contact with the

wall, Reese managed to roll Wallace off London and pull her up to her feet.

She threw herself into his arms.

"Are you all right?"

They asked the question in unison, then laughed with the giddy relief that came from having survived something deadly together.

In the background they heard the comforting sounds of police sirens approaching. It was over.

"I guess the superintendent got through," Reese told her. He continued holding her and didn't want to let her go. Ever.

A sigh racked her entire body. It was over. Finally over. She was free, really free. Free because of Reese. She owed him everything.

London drew back her head and saw the gash on the side of his forehead where he'd hit the wall. He *was* hurt. "Oh God, you're bleeding."

He touched the area gingerly. It was throbbing and felt to him as if it was three times the size of a normal head. He looked down at the blood on his fingers. "I guess I must have hit my head harder than I thought."

"Here, lean on me," she instructed, placing her shoulder beneath his arm.

He looked at her. She looked frazzled and beyond worn-out. This had been some ordeal for her. He should be the one holding her up.

"Maybe we can lean on each other," he suggested with a half smile.

She could have cried she was so relieved, so happy. "Sounds good to me."

* * *

"Feels like just yesterday that I was here," London murmured to Reese.

She was sitting up on a hospital bed in the far corner of the emergency room while Alix finished examining her. Refusing to go the usual route and change into a hospital gown, or even be separated from London, Reese was sitting on the chair beside her. The gash on his forehead had long since been attended to and was now covered with a bandage.

Reese laughed shortly. "Feels more like an eternity to me."

"The truth, as always, is somewhere in the middle," Alix commented diplomatically, putting down the instrument she'd used to check London's pupils one last time. "After scads of tests, the good news is that there's nothing wrong with you that a soak in a hot tub and a good night's sleep won't fix."

London continued to watch the other woman, waiting for the other shoe to drop. "And the bad news?"

Alix laughed for the first time since she'd heard that an ambulance had brought Reese and London in. She'd raced into the E.R. from the fourth floor the moment she knew, determined to be the one to attend them. Reese couldn't bully her into backing off.

She was nothing if not thorough, despite his protests. It was a relief to discover that neither was seriously hurt. Even Reese's head wound would heal nicely. There was no evidence of internal bleeding, no concussion. The prognosis couldn't have been better.

Alix looked at Reese. "It's obvious she's been hanging around you too long." She decided to oblige London and give her a downside. "The bad news is that I think the wedding dress is ruined."

London looked at the torn, dirty dress draped over the back of the chair. Her mouth turned grim. "Burn it."

Alix looked from London to Reese. She hadn't been privy to what had happened just before the ambulance had brought them here, hadn't really been able to talk to Reese since he'd shown her the ring he was going to give London two days ago.

She glanced at the woman's hand and saw that there was no ring on the proper finger. Had he asked her and she'd turned him down? Or was he still waiting for the "right" moment? Then why had she been brought in wearing a wedding dress?

Tactfully Alix said nothing. "I'll leave you two to get ready." She picked up both charts and made one last notation on London's. "You're both free to go."

London looked down at the hospital gown they'd had her put on. She couldn't leave in this and she refused to put the wedding dress on again. She turned her eyes toward Reese, a mute supplication in her eyes.

He picked up on it immediately. Even if she had been willing to don the dress again, he wouldn't have let her. The sooner that was out of her sight, the sooner she would really start to heal.

"Alix, you still keep an extra set of scrubs in your locker?"

Alix thought that an odd question at this time. "Yes, why?" And then she looked at London's face and understood. Sometime soon, Alix thought, she was going to corner Reese and get some answers. But not this afternoon. "Oh. Okay, sure. I'll bring them around in a few minutes," she promised.

Charts in hand, Alix slipped out, pulling the curtain closed around them, giving them a small measure of privacy in a nonprivate environment.

Restless, London laced her fingers together, then unlaced them. "She's nice."

"The best." Because his legs still felt a little wobbly, he remained seated. But he reached for her hand and wound his fingers protectively around it.

She smiled, the simple action warming her. "You two been friends long?"

He was feeling his way around. This was the first real conversation they'd had since he'd walked out of her apartment. "Long enough for me to show her the engagement ring."

She nodded. That explained the way Alix had looked at the wedding dress. A flood of guilt came over her. Again. Just as it had this morning and the night before. And the afternoon before that.

"Reese—"

"London—"

Their voices overlapped, blending together. London welcomed the reprieve. "You first," she said.

"Ladies first," he insisted, stalling for time, not knowing how to form the words that went with the emotions ricocheting around his heart.

He could have lost her today. Forever.

The realization echoed through him, stunning him with its power. It made him determined to put his ego aside and be in London's life, at least on the perimeter, at all costs.

In a way he supposed he could almost understand how Grant felt. He felt sorry for the man the police had arrested. But not sorry enough to regret that, from all indications, Wallace Grant was going to be put away for a long, long time. He wasn't going to be a threat to London anymore.

She took a deep breath. Her ribs ached from when Wallace had grabbed her this morning to keep her from fleeing the apartment. She found herself stumbling to get the right words into place.

"I was going to call you this morning and apologize about the other night—at least explain why I said what I did." She bit her lip. "I happened to mention to Wallace that you had proposed to me, and he must have panicked." She would never forget the look in his eyes. Like a child who had had his only toy taken away at Christmas. "He's been trying to work up the nerve to propose to me all this time."

How could she have been so blind? London berated herself. How could she not have seen any of this coming?

"He did," she told Reese in a small voice. "And he confessed about the roses and the notes. He sent them to make it look as if I was being stalked so that my father would keep him on, but he tried to do it so that I wouldn't be frightened." Her mouth curved in a sad smile. "He succeeded, you know. I wasn't afraid." She couldn't help it. Now that everything was settling down, she felt sorry for the man. "Wallace was really trying to look out for me."

There were tears in her eyes. She had an incredibly soft heart, Reese thought. Any other woman would have been full of anger for what she had been put through, not felt sorry for her stalker.

"London, he's a sick man."

"I know." She took another deep breath and let it out slowly. "Funny, isn't it? The only man who ever promised to stay in my life turns out to be a deranged stalker."

Reese stood up and came to her. "He's not the only one who wants to be in your life permanently, London."

She looked at Reese, searching his face. Trying to find answers to half-formed questions. "You mean you still do, even after all this?"

How could she possibly think his heart was so fickle? "Why would any of this change my desire to marry you? If anything, it just shows me that you need someone in your life to take care of you."

No, she wasn't going to be smothered. She didn't need a keeper. "I don't—"

"Yes," he told her firmly, cutting her off, "you do." This wasn't a point to be argued. "We all do." He took her hands into his. "We all need someone to take care of us and to take care of," he emphasized. "That's what marriage is supposed to be. A fifty-fifty deal. Sometimes it tips a little one way, sometimes the other, but in the end it levels out. You need some-one, London. Let it be me." He threaded his fingers through her hair, cupping her cheek. "Because I need you.

"I didn't realize it, didn't know I was missing any-thing, until you came into my life and showed me how drab it had been up until then. Until you showed me how good it could be. I want you to keep on showing me, London. Until we're both very, very old."

He made her smile. He always did. "Making love into our nineties?" She laughed softly. "They'll want to study us in a lab."

He shrugged. Loving her. Wanting her. "Let them. As long as we're there together, it doesn't matter where we are or who else is around." And then he grew serious. "I love you, London. And I want to be there for you. When you wake up in the morning. When you go to sleep at night. I want to be next to you."

The smile came into her eyes. "Tall order for a physician."

There were always ways around things. "I'll get people to cover."

But she shook her head. "I don't want you to be any different from the way you are right now." And then she smiled again. Broadly. "Maybe a little cleaner, but just as dedicated, just as good, just as sincere as you are this moment. Because that's the man I fell in love with." She stopped, surprised at herself. "Wow, I said it. I really said it." She looked at him to see if the significance had penetrated. "I said I love you."

It was going to be all right, he thought. From now on it was going to be all right. "No, technically you said 'fell in love with.' But there's no penalty. You get a do-over if you want to say it right this time."

Oh, God, why had she waited so long? This feeling of loving someone, of loving him, was so overwhelming, so wonderful as it rushed through her, freeing her.

"I want to say it right every time." She framed his face with her hands. "I love you, Dr. Bendenetti. Very, very much." She brushed a kiss against his lips. "So much that it scares me. That's why I said no."

Amusement entered his eyes. "So if you loved me less, you would have said yes?"

She laughed, knowing she had to sound like a crazy person. But that was okay. Love could make you crazy sometimes and she was ready for that. "No. But if that offer of yours is still on the table, I'd like to take it this time. I'd like to say yes now."

Definitely all right, he thought, relieved. "It's still on the table."

"Yes now," she echoed, and then laughed. He put his arms around her, and she winced slightly, then shifted. Away from the pain and into him. "New bruises on top of the old ones. I guess the bride's going to be wearing black and blue."

He was looking forward to caring for those bruises. "That's okay. Haven't you heard? I'm a very good doctor."

If her heart was any more full, it was going to explode. "Yes, I have heard that."

He drew her a little closer. "And as long as the bride is mine, I don't care if she shows up at the wedding in Technicolor."

"Oh, the bride is yours, all right." London wrapped her arms around his neck and brought her lips up to his. "The bride is very yours."

Alix parted the curtain on the side, the scrubs she'd gone to fetch for London in her hand. She stopped short and then quietly placed the scrubs on the bed, fairly certain that her presence had not been detected by either of her two patients. They were very busy wrapped up in each other and the kiss they were sharing.

She smiled to herself as she slipped out. Looked like Reese had finally gotten around to proposing.

*   *   *   *   *

INTIMATE MOMENTS™
presents:

Romancing the Crown

With the help of their powerful allies, the royal family of Montebello is determined to find their missing heir. But the search for the beloved prince is not without danger—or passion!

Available in September 2002:
A ROYAL MURDER
by Lyn Stone (IM #1172)

Murder brought beautiful Nina Caruso to Montebello in search of justice. But would her love for sexy P.I. Ryan McDonough help open her eyes to the shocking truth behind her brother's death?

This exciting series continues throughout the year with these fabulous titles:

Available only from Silhouette Intimate Moments at your favorite retail outlet.

Silhouette®
Where love comes alive™

Visit Silhouette at www.eHarlequin.com

SIMRC9

From award-winning author
Marie Ferrarella:

Meet *The Bachelors of Blair Memorial*—

Dr. Lukas Graywolf: Lover, Healer and Hero in
IN GRAYWOLF'S HANDS
(IM #1155) On Sale June 2002

Dr. Reese Bendenetti: Lone Wolf,
Doctor and Protector in
M.D. MOST WANTED
(IM #1167) On Sale August 2002

Dr. Harrison "Mac" MacKenzie: M.D.,
Bad Boy and Charmer in
MAC'S BEDSIDE MANNER
(SE #1492) On Sale September 2002

Dr. Terrance McCall: Doctor in Disguise
and Secret Agent in
UNDERCOVER M.D.
(IM #1191) On Sale December 2002

Don't miss this exciting new series!

Available at your favorite retail outlet.

Where love comes alive™

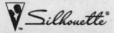

 Silhouette®

COMING NEXT MONTH

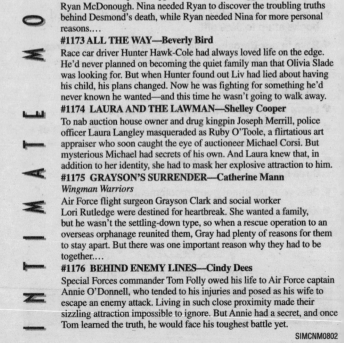

#1171 THE WAY TO YESTERDAY—Sharon Sala

Mary Faith O'Rourke lost everything when her husband and infant daughter died in a car crash outside their Savannah home. For years Mary felt responsible. She longed for a second chance, and when fate led her to a ring with mysterious powers, she thought she'd found one. But had her dream actually come true, or was the real nightmare just beginning?

#1172 A ROYAL MURDER—Lyn Stone

Romancing the Crown

When Nina Caruso learned that her half brother, Desmond, had been killed, she headed for the kingdom of Montebello to see that justice was done. She expected opposition but not the rugged royal P.I. Ryan McDonough. Nina needed Ryan to discover the troubling truths behind Desmond's death, while Ryan needed Nina for more personal reasons....

#1173 ALL THE WAY—Beverly Bird

Race car driver Hunter Hawk-Cole had always loved life on the edge. He'd never planned on becoming the quiet family man that Olivia Slade was looking for. But when Hunter found out Liv had lied about having his child, his plans changed. Now he was fighting for something he'd never known he wanted—and this time he wasn't going to walk away.

#1174 LAURA AND THE LAWMAN—Shelley Cooper

To nab auction house owner and drug kingpin Joseph Merrill, police officer Laura Langley masqueraded as Ruby O'Toole, a flirtatious art appraiser who soon caught the eye of auctioneer Michael Corsi. But mysterious Michael had secrets of his own. And Laura knew that, in addition to her identity, she had to mask her explosive attraction to him.

#1175 GRAYSON'S SURRENDER—Catherine Mann

Wingman Warriors

Air Force flight surgeon Grayson Clark and social worker Lori Rutledge were destined for heartbreak. She wanted a family, but he wasn't the settling-down type, so when a rescue operation to an overseas orphanage reunited them, Gray had plenty of reasons for them to stay apart. But there was one important reason why they had to be together....

#1176 BEHIND ENEMY LINES—Cindy Dees

Special Forces commander Tom Folly owed his life to Air Force captain Annie O'Donnell, who tended to his injuries and posed as his wife to escape an enemy attack. Living in such close proximity made their sizzling attraction impossible to ignore. But Annie had a secret, and once Tom learned the truth, he would face his toughest battle yet.

SIMCNM0802